The Casseveti Inheritance

Three siblings. Two families. One explosive will!

When billionaire James Casseveti dies, his business is split between the two children he abandoned from his first marriage and the daughter of his second. Siblings who've never even met! Can love reunite a family at war?

Ava Casseveti's father wants her to make amends for a wrong he did his former business partner. Will agreeing to help his son lead to a happy-ever-after?

Bitter at his father's betrayal, Luca Petrovelli has vowed never to fall in love. But can a marriage of convenience change his mind?

Overcome with grief, Jodie Petrovelli finds herself in the arms of her own Prince Charming. Can their secret baby unite them—forever?

Dear Reader,

This book was written just before times became tumultuous and as such it feels important to me.

I really enjoyed writing this book about two people who have never met, yet their pasts intertwine and connect them and bring them together. As Ava and Liam open up to each other, they realize their connection is very present and cannot be ignored— however much they might want to. And believe me, they try!

I hope you enjoy reading how love managed to sneak in under their radar and navigate them toward a future together and a permanent connection.

Nina x

Italian Escape with the CEO

—

Nina Milne

HARLEQUIN

Romance

Recycling programs
for this product may
not exist in your area.

ISBN-13: 978-1-335-56689-8

Italian Escape with the CEO

Copyright © 2021 by Nina Milne

This edition published by arrangement with Harlequin Books S.A.

For questions and comments about the quality of this book, please contact us at CustomerService@Harlequin.com.

Harlequin Enterprises ULC
22 Adelaide St. West, 40th Floor
Toronto, Ontario M5H 4E3, Canada
www.Harlequin.com

Printed in U.S.A.

Nina Milne has always dreamed of writing for Harlequin Romance—ever since she played libraries with her mother's stacks of Harlequin novels as a child. On her way to this dream, Nina acquired an English degree, a hero of her own, three gorgeous children and—somehow!—an accountancy qualification. She lives in Brighton and has filled her house with stacks of books—her very own *real* library.

Books by Nina Milne

Harlequin Romance

A Crown by Christmas

Their Christmas Royal Wedding

The Derwent Family

Rafael's Contract Bride
The Earl's Snow-Kissed Proposal
Claimed by the Wealthy Magnate

Claiming His Secret Royal Heir
Marooned with the Millionaire
Conveniently Wed to the Prince
Hired Girlfriend, Pregnant Fiancée?
Whisked Away by Her Millionaire Boss
Baby on the Tycoon's Doorstep

Visit the Author Profile page
at Harlequin.com for more titles.

To my family and friends—you are all very precious to me.

CHAPTER ONE

AVA CASSEVETI STUDIED her reflection in the mirror and tried out her trademark smile. *Fake it till you make it.* It was a mantra that had always served her well, had got her through an outwardly gilded life, and one that she now relied on to manage the trials and tribulations that had multiplied on a daily basis since her father's death.

Another look at herself and she reached out for her reddest lipstick, a fire-engine red, completely suited to the day ahead. With any luck people would be distracted from the tiredness in her eyes, the pallor of her skin that even her super-expensive, perfectly matched foundation couldn't completely conceal.

But she would keep it together, present the façade, convince the world that she was in control, a competent businesswoman able to hold the family company together.

Family. The word boomed around her head, clanged with irony as the complications of her family tree threatened to tangle her mind.

Why did you do it, Dad?

She closed her eyes, pictured her father, the bluff good looks, the boyish cheek he had maintained even into his sixties, the youthfulness that had survived his first heart attack four years before. His presence, his aura, her belief in him, all shattered when she'd learnt the contents of his will, her grief at losing the man she adored darkened by the confusion and hurt over his betrayal, wrapped in the legalese of his last will and testament.

Because instead of leaving Dolci, the dessert company he had founded, to Ava—the company she had put her heart and soul into for the past five years—he had left it to Ava *and* her two half-siblings, Luca and Jodi. Remembered shock, disbelief and the ice-cold stab of betrayal hit her again.

Luca and Jodi Petrovelli, children from his previous marriage, from his past, who had never been part of the Dolci venture. Children who hadn't even kept the Casseveti surname, instead had taken their mother's. Luca and Jodi, adults now, whom Ava had never even met. Though she had known of their existence, the shadowy threat of her childhood nightmares. Little surprise really—even now she could hear her mother's dire warnings.

'We have to be careful, Ava darling. Always. Those people would do anything to get Daddy back. And we won't let that happen, will we, sweetheart?'

Three-year-old Ava had shaken her head vigorously, her mouth dry with fear as she'd imagined Luca and Jodi kidnapping her father.

'So we'll be perfect, darling. A perfect family for Daddy. We have to be perfect.'

And Ava had watched Karen Casseveti reach for her make-up.

So that had become Ava's mission: achieve perfection to ensure a perfect family so the perfidious Petrovellis wouldn't take her father away. Her understanding was hazy but absolute as she grew into an implicit alliance with her mother—a joint determination that James Casseveti *would* stay with *this* family. Though there was always that doubt—after all, he had walked out on his previous wife and children, the precedent set. The doubts were worsened by the overheard conversations that permeated her consciousness as she grew older, the tears and recriminations from her mother.

'You never loved me. You still love her.

Would you have married me if I didn't have money?'

Her father's muted, soothing answers that eventually culminated in exasperation and finally into goaded admission.

'I did love her and Luca—of course I did. They were my family. But now you've got me, we have a marriage, we have a daughter. Why can't that be enough? This is our life.'

And Ava had come to realise that her father had loved his first wife, but had left her regardless, had decided that wealth and connections trumped family. She'd wondered if he ever regretted it, wondered if she and Karen were second best, if the riches and success could compensate.

So she'd redoubled her efforts. Ava always looked perfect, acted perfectly, danced to the tune her mother played. In truth there was no need for complaint. Her life had been one of privilege and she knew how lucky she was.

Yet there had been times when the constraints had stifled her individuality, when she'd felt almost like a parody of her own creation—an impeccable mix of English aristocracy and Dolci heiress. She'd wanted a life where she could follow her own dreams, not those concocted for her, a life not governed by press and publicity and the need to be flawless.

Yet in the end, despite everything, Luca and Jodi had indeed been a threat to be feared; Ava had not been perfect enough and now her half-siblings once more threatened her peace. Two shadowy figures who refused to meet her, refused to communicate except through lawyers.

Ava pulled open a drawer on her dressing table, took out the letter she had read and re-read so many times in the past months. The letter of explanation her father had left her.

Dear Ava
I know you must be hurt and angry, and I hope this letter will mitigate that in some way. Please believe that I love you. You have been the most precious thing in my life these past years. You showed me, proved to me, that I am capable of being a good father. You have done nothing wrong.

You did nothing wrong, Ava, but I did. I left behind another family, a wife I loved, a son I loved. Luca was five when I left and my wife Therese was pregnant with a daughter I have never met, Jodi.

However much I try to justify my de-

*cisions now, towards the end of my life,
I know that they were wrong. I left my
life with them to live a life of wealth and
plenty, to achieve the success I craved.
But Luca and Jodi are my family, my
children, and as such they deserve a
part in this family company. They should
have been given that opportunity a long
time ago.*

*I hope you can accept this and for-
give me.*

Ava placed the letter down and resisted the
urge to rub her eyes, knew tears would simply necessitate a touch-up of the carefully ap-
plied eye shadow, the mascara that enhanced
her already long eyelashes.

Her gaze flicked to her father's familiar
scrawl and she sighed—talk of acceptance
and forgiveness was all very well but that
wasn't how real life was panning out. For
a start Karen Casseveti had no intention
of doing either. Her whole life was focused
now on revenge for her husband's betrayal.
All she wanted to do was overturn the will
and oust the Petrovellis. Ava's refusal to do
that had caused a rift between them. Karen
could not comprehend her daughter's 'defi-
ance'. Guilt touched Ava—she understood

how her mother felt but knew that legally they didn't stand a chance. Knew that morally it wasn't the right thing to do. Yet she hated seeing her mother's bitterness and grief, even as she understood it. All through her marriage Karen had known that her husband still loved his first wife, but she'd concealed the knowledge, spun it into a sugar-coated illusion. In death James had torn that down, ripped away the gossamer strands to reveal the stark ugly truth.

As for Luca—who owned his own incredibly successful chocolate company—he seemed set on demonstrating just how little Dolci meant to him. He was refusing to engage, claimed that his sister was unsure of how to proceed and until she made up her mind, he would do nothing. In the meantime that left Dolci floundering in a mire of uncertainty, the Casseveti 'family' brand indelibly tainted, negative publicity and salacious gossip everywhere Ava looked, along with the damning verdict of the business world: that Ava Casseveti didn't have what it took. She was an ex-model, given a role in the company due to nepotism not ability. Otherwise why would her father have left the company to children he didn't even know?

Her perfectly manicured and painted nails

curled into her palms as determination to
prove everyone wrong clashed with the cas-
cade of self-doubt. After all, it was a valid
point—whatever he claimed in his letter her
father wouldn't have left two thirds of Dolci to
his other children if he truly believed in Ava.

But this morning wasn't about that.

Today was about the next part of her father's letter.

*There is another wrong I did, Ava.
One I haven't had the courage to rectify
myself and so I ask you to do it for me.*

*Many years ago, when I was still with
Therese, I had a friend and colleague
named Terry Rourke, and it was he and
I who came up with the idea of Dolci. It
was a pipe dream, discussed over a pint
of beer or a Sunday barbecue. I had no
legal obligation to bring him in on it but
I did have a moral one.*

*I believe Terry has passed away, but
he leaves behind a son—please do something for him in my name.*

*Thank you, Ava. I ask you to show un-
derstanding to your siblings and support
to your mother.*

My love
Dad

Sometimes it felt to Ava as if she had never known her father, that her relationship with him had been an illusion, a con, a dream, and it was only in death that he was showing his true colours. Yet whatever his shortcomings she missed him with an ache of grief that seared and swelled inside her even six months after his death. A grief that made her determined to at least try to carry out his wishes. James Casseveti had wanted Luca and Jodi to be involved in Dolci—Ava had to give them that chance And now she would go and try to make amends for a wrong done before she was even born.

One last look at her reflection and Ava gave a satisfied nod. She was as ready as she would ever be—ready to face Liam Rourke, Terry Rourke's son. Another fun day in the life of Ava Casseveti.

In his sleekly furnished office, a careful mix of minimalist and comfort, designed to inspire client confidence, Liam Rourke read the email on his screen. Surprise and disappointment coalesced into a low but heartfelt curse—he'd lost the Daley contract. For an instant anger joined the mix but he resisted the urge to slam his fist onto his desk. He couldn't win them all, he knew that. But this one stung, because he'd lost it to a man he knew and despised.

Andrew Joseph Mason, known to his upper-class pals as AJ. AJ Mason, ex-army like Liam. Founder of a security company. Like Liam. And there the parallels ended. AJ Mason came from 'proper' gilded army stock. There had been a Mason in the British army since time immemorial. No doubt since the first battalion of cavemen faced each other. And no doubt even millennia before they had been officer material, clad in a more expensive brand of leopard skin.

Now here was AJ Mason muscling in on his turf and Liam knew exactly how he was doing it. AJ had influence, clout and connections. All of which were undeniably impressive, especially when put against Liam's, which were pretty much non-existent. Liam had no army officers in his family, didn't have that extended familial network. But that shouldn't matter—though it had to AJ.

For a moment, memories hit Liam, of officer training thirteen years before, and the hell AJ Mason and a couple of his thuggish friends had put him through. AJ had taken an instant dislike to Liam, an antipathy born of his belief that officers should come from an upper-class background. A dislike that had flourished because Liam had turned out to be *first-class* officer material, had excelled in the training and exercises, had showed AJ up again and again. So AJ had exacted revenge; he'd known Liam would never 'snitch', so he and his friends had caused him to be ostracised, forced him to endure humiliation time and again.

Well, he wouldn't take it again. He was no longer a vulnerable eighteen-year-old boy. He'd figured out a way to beat AJ then and he'd do the same now. Years ago he'd managed to persuade AJ to meet him in the boxing ring. Once there he'd won a hard-fought victory, one where he'd showed AJ up and beaten him fair and square, the land of each punch a relish and retaliation for the humiliations piled upon him. A relish he could still taste now.

But it was a defeat that had left AJ a laughing stock—worse, it had also come to the attention of senior army officers who had been less than happy with him despite his illustrious background and family. AJ had been livid at the time and it seemed that had festered over the years.

There was a knock on the door and Liam's PA pushed it open and entered.

'Hey, Rita.'

'Hey. I'm sorry about Daley.' The petite redhead shook her head. 'It sucks. I heard on the grapevine that AJ invited Old Man Daley over for dinner, brought out the family silver and had his wife name-drop like crazy. The tipping point was a promise to invite his daughter to the Henley regatta with a few minor royals in tow. Worse I heard AJ's going for the Beaumont contract too.'

Liam's jaw clenched. Beaumont Industries replaced their security providers every five years and had requested a tender from Rourke Securities. It would be the contract that took his business to the next level.

Rita hesitated. 'It gets worse.'

'Explain.'

'He's dropping insinuations as well as names over the port and cigars. About how tragic it was that you lost your wife. That the tragedy made you lose your edge and isn't it sad you can't bring yourself to even date anyone. Shows what a long way you are from recovery.'

The idea that AJ was using Jessica's death caused cold, hard anger to slide into his gut. Made worse as he realised the effectiveness of the tactic. Right or wrong, like it or not, clients wanted a man with edge to be in charge of their security contracts, not a man still swimming the depths of grief and guilt.

The ache of guilt, the sadness of what might have been, still pulsed inside him, part of the fabric of his being even though it was five years since Jess's death. The knowledge that their marriage had been a disaster of his own making, that he had taken her love and given her nothing back, allowed her to waste her tragically short life on him.

The start of their relationship had been overshadowed by the illness and death of his father. Followed by their hasty marriage due to Jess's belief she was pregnant, though by that point Liam had already suspected their relationship was doomed. That in his grief he'd mistaken attraction and liking for love. That Jess's love for him had blinded him and made him believe he felt the same way. But Jess had been so happy, so grateful even, that she had touched his heart and so he'd squashed down the niggle of doubt, the growing realisation that he didn't love her. Besides, he would never abandon a child. And by the time they'd realised the pregnancy scare was a false one he'd known he couldn't reject her love, couldn't hurt her the way his mother had hurt his father.

A few years later Jess had fallen ill and her

last words to him had been of love, an admonishment not to grieve for too long and not to feel guilt over their marriage. Perhaps her forgiveness should have absolved him but in some ways it simply weighted the load more. That final conversation had torn his heart, shredded his insides with sadness and frustration. He would have done anything to give Jess more time, a chance to follow her dreams instead of waiting for him to return her love.

But he wouldn't show anyone that pain and he knew damn well it hadn't caused him to lose his edge. 'Thanks for the info,' he said. 'I'll deal with it.'

'I know you will.' Rita glanced at her watch. 'Anyways, the other reason I came up here was to tell you that you have a visitor.'

'A potential client?'

'I assume so.' Rita frowned. 'She looks familiar but she's wearing sunglasses and a scarf. Didn't want to give me her full name either.' None of this was unusual—sometimes clients were loath to give their identity or be recognised. 'She just said her name is Ava.'

Ava. It took all of Liam's iron control not to react, even as he told himself he was being foolish. Ava wasn't that uncommon a name—yet to him it had huge significance. The name bandied about during his childhood: Ava

Casseveti—daughter of the man who had betrayed his father, driven Terry Rourke to drink and bitterness.

Liam gave his head a small shake—there were plenty of Avas in the world. And why on earth would Ava Casseveti show her face here? Any Casseveti was definitively persona non grata in his world. 'Bring her in.'

Rita nodded and exited the room. Liam rose, paced, worked to clear his mind from thoughts of the past.

A minute later there was a brief knock, the door swung open and Rita showed a woman in. Designer sunglasses hid her eyes and a scarf covered her hair; her clothes were an explicit demonstration of her status. Clearly expensive, without being flamboyant, they combined power with chic. White blouse, long-sleeved and V-necked, tucked into a dark checked skirt that emphasised her slender waist and long legs. Cool, sleek, professional.

Liam rose and headed round the desk as Rita made a discreet exit. 'Liam Rourke,' he said.

Before he could hold out his hand the woman deftly removed her sunglasses, dropped them into her shoulder bag, then swiftly tugged off the scarf to reveal long glossy corn-blonde hair that fell in perfect waves to frame a heart-shaped face. But what arrested him most were her eyes. They were an extraordinary colour, a luminous amber flecked with copper. To his chagrin his jaw dropped of its own volition. There was no need for her to identify herself. This was definitely Ava Casseveti and she was stunning. Little wonder that a few years back she'd taken the modelling world by storm. He blinked and forced his brain cells to regroup.

'Ava Casseveti,' she said and held her hand out—long-fingered and elegant, silver rings on the first finger of her right hand and the middle of her left, perfect nails a pale brown. Liam shook her hand, registered the smooth silk of her skin and a sudden little zing shot through him at her touch. *Whoa.* His gaze met hers and for a fleeting second he saw a flicker of shock in the amber depths and he knew she'd felt it too.

Time to focus, however surreal this felt. But it was hard because in some strange way Ava had always been a part of his life, both a nemesis and a motivator. Hadn't he wanted to prove to his father, *to himself*, that he would succeed despite what James Casseveti had done? Driven to do better than James Casseveti's daughter.

All of which explained that jolt and presumably also explained why their hands were still intertwined. As if she too realised that fact she moved backwards and disengaged her clasp, inhaled deeply and met his gaze. 'Thank you for seeing me at such short notice. Before I explain why I am here, can I ask if your father ever mentioned my father?'

The words tumbled from generous lips outlined in the reddest of reds and the sheer irony of the question nearly startled a bitter laugh from him. Instead he merely inclined his head. 'Yes. He did.' On a daily basis. The story of James Casseveti's betrayal had been the equivalent of Liam's bedtime story, the tale of how Terry Rourke's best friend had used *their* business idea to leapfrog to fame and fortune. And that act of treachery had destroyed his father's life, his marriage, his job...the success of Dolci had broken Terry Rourke. And broken his family with it.

Pulling himself to the present, he gestured to his desk. 'Why don't you sit down? Then you can tell me why you are here.'

CHAPTER TWO

AVA MOVED TOWARDS the chair Liam had indicated, tried to use the time to regroup, refocus, settle the thrum of her nerves. Wished she could figure out what the hell was going on. *Quit kidding yourself, Ava.* She knew exactly what was going on. For some inexplicable, unfair reason her hormones had decided to awaken from dormancy and fix their attention on Liam Rourke.

To be fair the man was gorgeous. Thick coppery brown hair, a face that held strength and determination in its clean planes and angles, firm lips and a body that combined lithe muscle, breadth and length and... And jeez what was she doing? An inventory? This was not what she was here for. She sank onto the state-of-the-art chair, prayed he hadn't noticed her practically measure him up with her eyes and pulled her thoughts together into the carefully rehearsed words.

'I want you to know that during his lifetime my father never mentioned your family to me. Not once. However he left me a letter to be opened after his death. In it he explained that he did your father a moral wrong. Apparently they discussed the idea for a company like Dolci together and therefore he felt it was morally incorrect of him to set up Dolci without any reference to your father.' She paused and continued, kept her voice even. 'I would like to stress that there is no legal obligation at play here. There was no partnership, no agreement and no legal need for my father to involve yours.'

'So why are you here?' A hard edge of anger lined his words and she couldn't blame him. 'Given legal obligations clearly trump moral responsibility.'

'I didn't say that. I'm here because my father did feel a moral responsibility, but I'd be a fool not to safeguard my company. I want to be clear I'd like to offer compensation without prejudice. I'd like to carry out my father's wish to make amends.'

'How noble of him.' Liam made no attempt to hide the sarcasm. 'Unfortunately he is too late. My father died ten years ago and the damage was done.'

'I'm sorry.' And she was, she had hoped

against hope that Terry Rourke had been unaffected by her father's actions, but the anger, the bitter twist of Liam's lips belied that hope. Showed her the utter inadequacy of her words.

In an instant, though, his face donned a mask of cool neutrality. 'An apology won't help my dad now—you cannot compensate for what your father did.'

'There must be something.'

'Such as?' The question was cold and tinged with contempt.

Yet it was imperative she carried out her father's wishes; she knew she couldn't just slough this responsibility off. Knew she didn't want to. 'What about the rest of your family? Is there anything I can do for them?'

'No.' The syllable was instant and absolute and she saw a shadow cross his eyes 'My mother has remarried and she is happy—I will not let you charge in and dredge up old memories to make yourself feel better.'

'That is not why I am doing this.' Now anger surfaced and she glared at him, saw the clench of his jaw. 'I want to do something to atone for what my father did. That is what he wanted.'

'Then why didn't he do it?'

It was a good question and one she didn't

want to answer. Truth be told her father had *always* been morally weak. He would have intended to make amends but he would have easily talked himself out of it, put it off, procrastinated. 'That is irrelevant now. He asked me to act for him and that's what I want to do.'

'You can't. Accept it. And accept that I don't want your bounty—because nothing can atone for that betrayal. His perfidy broke my father. He felt cheated and bitter, a bitterness that pervaded and corroded his life. He began to drink heavily, he lost his job, his marriage fell apart as he watched your father climb the scale of success and fame. I understand that he could have made different choices, but the choices he made were put into play by your father.'

Ava winced, felt her face scrunch, her body braced in an attempt to reject his words even as she recognised their truth and realised the impact this must have had on Liam. Then for a second she saw something flash across his face. A sudden shaft of sympathy that vanished before she could be sure it was there. 'I... I... I don't know what to say.'

'Then say nothing. This is not your fault— I understand that.' He rubbed his hand over the back of his neck and exhaled. 'But there is nothing you can do to "right the wrong". The man your father wronged is gone. This is too little too late. The best thing you can do now is leave.'

Ava nodded, realised that her very presence must be dredging up memories for *him*. She rose and he followed suit, walked round the desk to usher her towards the door. Halfway there she stopped. 'Hang on.' Ava turned, reached into her bag and pulled out a card. 'Here. This…' The words dried up, and they both seemed to freeze. Her feet felt stuck as his sudden unexpected proximity assailed her. The scent of his aftershave with its woodsy overtone tantalised her, and for one moment her gaze snagged and held on his lips, the firm etched outline of them. What was she *doing*? Gritting her teeth, Ava tucked a determined tendril of hair behind her ear and then continued, annoyed that the slightest of wobbles tremored the words. 'This has my details on it. I know I can't make up for what my father did but if I can ever do you a favour, please get in touch.'

Not that that was likely to happen. 'I mean it.' She held the card out, saw his hesitation, wondered if he was as unsettled as she. Carefully he took the card, but despite his care his fingers brushed hers and there it was again, a frisson, and this time she was sure he felt it too, saw awareness jolt in the depths of his cobalt eyes.

'Sure,' he said, though she suspected he'd bin the card as soon as she left.

Without meeting his gaze she slipped on her sunglasses and headed for the door.

Two weeks later

Liam scrolled down his inbox, each email sending his anger up a notch.

Given the report in the financial press I have concerns…

As a result of the uncertainties facing your firm…

Hi, Liam. I just wanted to check in, mate. See if you're OK. I'm sorry to hear you haven't been well. Grief over the loss of a loved one is so hard and it's fine if you need some time off.

Anger slammed him. 'Uncertainties' and 'time off', his backside. Over the past two weeks AJ's smear campaign had escalated, cast a tightening net of doubt over Rourke Securities by targeting its CEO. He'd done all the sensible things so far, looked at the legal route, decided not to react as that might give credence to the rumours. But enough was enough.

He snagged his jacket from the back of his chair and left the office and an hour later he pushed through the glass revolving door that led to the plush lobby of AJ Security, headed towards the reception area and smiled his friendliest smile.

'Good afternoon. I was wondering if you could help me.' He pulled out his army credentials and flashed them at the receptionist. 'I'm a fellow officer of AJ's—we trained together at Sandhurst—could I run up and surprise him?'

The receptionist looked doubtful. 'I'm only a temp here. I'm not sure...'

Another smile. 'I promise he won't mind. But just in case I'll tell him you tried to stop me. Would that work?'

'Um...' Before the temp could say anything Liam headed purposefully for the lift, saw the temp press a button on the phone and start to talk. He hopped out at the first floor and glanced round the open-plan office, then strode purposefully through the line of desks until he spotted a door with AJ's name plate, guarded by a PA. The blond man rose to his feet. 'Excuse me, sir. I need you to stop right there.'

'Not happening.' Liam knew he needed to move fast. 'I just want a quick word with AJ.'

'I'm afraid that won't be possible.'

'We'll see.'

Before the man could do anything Liam vaulted over the desk and in seconds had the PA's hands behind his back. 'I'm sorry about this and I really don't want to hurt you. I'll be a few minutes, that's all.'

The man nodded and stood and watched as Liam released him and headed for the office door, pushed it open and entered. He turned and stood with his back against it, estimating he had a few minutes at best before security guards burst in.

'Hey, AJ.'

AJ's eyes were wide and satisfaction slid through Liam as he saw fear flash in their depths. 'What do you want, Rourke?'

'Call off your guards and I'll tell you. Or...' and now Liam stepped forward '...let's do this the old-fashioned way and see who wins. It didn't take me that long last time to kick your butt.' He eyed the other man with contempt. 'And you were in better shape then. So make your choice.'

AJ picked the phone up. 'It's all right, guys. I've got this.'

'Good choice. I'm here to say back off.'

'Back off what?' The upper-class drawl grated on his nerves but Liam kept a smile on his face.

'Back off my clients and my business.'

Now AJ spread his arms in a gesture of innocence. 'I'm not doing anything, Rourke. If I have a bit of chat with my potential clients about your very understandable grief over your wife's tragic death, that's my prerogative.'

'Leave my wife out of this.' Rage threatened and he tamped it down into a useable commodity. Took a step forward, fists clenched, saw panic cross AJ's face as he pushed his chair backwards.

'Sorry. Sorry.' Now he pressed a button under his desk. 'But the Beaumont contract will be mine. And there's nothing you can do to stop me.'

'Watch me, Andrew, just watch me. You're a coward who relies on Daddy's money and position. Always were, always will be. Much as I'd love to wipe that smirk off your face, I'm not going to. This time let's finish it in the business ring. The result will be the same.'

Liam turned and exited, walked back to the lift, descended and left through the revolving door. Adrenalin surged through his body and he unclenched his fists. There was no way he would let AJ Mason win this and take Rourke Securities down.

Whatever it took, Liam would win. As he climbed into his car his mind raced through options. Legal and IT routes were all very well but the most important part of his strategy was to show Ray Beaumont and everyone else out there that Liam Rourke was on the top of his game, in control and capable. He needed to combat, not only AJ's accusations, but also the force of his connections and lifestyle, which would impress and bedazzle Ray Beaumont and his wife.

He drummed his fingers on his steering wheel, and an idea niggled the corner of his brain, grew and expanded into a plan as he completed the drive back to Rourke HQ. A plan he recognised as a gamble that verged on the cusp of insane. But one thing he'd learnt in the army was that sometimes the risky way was the only way to go, however high the stakes.

Once in his office he lifted the keyboard on his desk and pulled out Ava Casseveti's card. Studied it for a long moment. Daughter of aristocracy, ex-model, businesswoman, celebrity... Beautiful, charming, intelligent, well connected... And she owed him. Could he ask a favour of an enemy? In these circumstances, yes, he could.

Decision made, he punched in her number.

One ring, two, and then the call was picked up. 'Hello.'

'Ava. It's Liam Rourke.'

A couple of beats of silence and then, 'Liam. Good to hear from you.' Her tone clearly belied the truth of the sentiment.

'You said to call if I thought of a favour you could do me. Well, I have.'

There was a silence, then, 'Go ahead.'

'I'd rather pitch this in person. How about dinner tonight? I can pick you up from work if you like?'

'Um…' Liam realised he was holding his breath, told himself if Ava refused then he'd come up with an alternative strategy. 'OK. But I'll meet you there. Just tell me the location.'

'I'll text details and how about we meet at eight?' He'd already picked the perfect place, the right backdrop to help explain his plan, a venue that also had the merit of getting him seen in the right circles.

'I'll be there.'

A few hours later Liam approached the restaurant, as a taxi pulled up to the kerb. He waited and watched as Ava alighted from the black cab. His breath hitched in his throat—she looked…stunning. Her blonde hair was up in an elegant sweep that highlighted her slanted cheekbones; she wore a simple fitted black dress made that little bit different by the subtle striped detail of the V neck.

She paid the driver and headed towards him, her poise still reminiscent of the catwalk, graceful and lithe. As she reached him he nodded. 'Thank you for coming.'

'No problem. I told you to call if you needed a favour.'

'Then let's go in and I'll explain.'

He stepped back to allow her to go first, forced his gaze away from the slender column of her neck, the tantalising sweep of bare skin, focused instead on the air above her head. That at least was safe. Once inside he signed them in, and led the way into the restaurant situated on the ground floor of the exclusive military club.

Ava glanced around the room, her amber eyes scanning the huge portraits of historic military figures on the walls, the plush leather theme of the room reminiscent of men's clubs from days gone by. 'The website said it's imposing and they were right. But it also feels as though it is a part of history.'

Liam nodded. 'The army, battles, war have been part of life for centuries. This gives people a place to be part of that community if they want to be.'

'Do you come here a lot, then?'

'No. I use it to meet clients sometimes. Particularly if they have an army background, or find this sort of thing impressive.'

'So why did you ask me here?'

'Well, partly because the food is incredible. And partly for a reason that will become clear later.' He wanted to be seen with Ava, wanted the news to trickle back to AJ and his clients.

'I did have a look at the menu online,' she said. 'For all the different restaurants. They all look great—I didn't think a military club would have a tea room. Though it looks amazing with the book-lined walls. The cream teas did look good too.'

'It sounds like you studied the website pretty thoroughly.'

'Absolutely. I like to be prepared.'

'Rather than surprised?'

'I'm not keen on surprises. Plus if I hadn't prepared how would I have known what to wear? Imagine if I hadn't checked and I'd turned up in a gold lamé cocktail dress.'

Startled, he glanced at her. 'You own a gold lamé cocktail dress?'

'That's for me to know.' Her smile was almost shy and he realised that somehow they had relaxed into easy conversation. The knowledge unsettled him—this was Ava Casseveti, daughter of his father's nemesis—it shouldn't be easy to talk to her.

He gestured to the menus. 'I guess we'd better choose our food. Then we can get down to business.'

She studied the menu, took her time and then gave a small decisive nod. 'I'll go for Chalk Stream trout and buttered kale and dauphinoise potatoes. What about you?'

'The oven-roasted duck with roast potatoes and broccoli. Would you like wine?'

'Yes, please. White for me. I'm happy for you to choose.'

A waiter glided up, so silent and discreet that as always Liam wondered how it was done, was tempted to ask to see the soles of the man's shoes, check if they were crepe. Indeed, discretion was the order of the day. The restaurant was busy but the tables were well placed and the music pitched so that it wasn't possible to hear more than a general hum of conversation.

Within minutes the waiter returned. Liam declined to go through the tasting rigmarole and the waiter poured the delicate golden wine into the crystal glasses before melting away once more.

They sipped the wine and both nodded approval at the same moment and then Ava placed her glass down. 'Tell me the favour.'

Liam took a deep breath. This was it. Time to put Campaign Insanity into play and let the chips fall where they would.

CHAPTER THREE

Ava TOOK A sip from her wine, savoured the floral overtone as it trickled down her throat. Studied Liam's expression and wondered what on earth he could be about to request. Premonition tickled the back of her neck—instinct warned that perhaps she should do a runner now. Yet she couldn't stop herself from lingering on the strength of his features, the line and shape of his lips.

He leant back slightly, his body relaxed though this was belied by a tension in his jaw and the guarded look in his eyes. 'As you know, I head up Rourke Securities.'

Ava nodded. Her research had shown her that his company was a massive success. Both admiration and envy tingled through her. This man had forged his own fortune—come up the hard way. Like Luca Petrovelli. And unlike Ava. Ava had been born into advantage and ready-made fame, her mother a Lady, a minor royal celebrity, her father founder and CEO of Dolci, rolling in success and riches. What would she have achieved in Liam's shoes or in Luca's? She pushed the thoughts away, focused instead on Liam. 'Go on.'

'In recent weeks I've hit a snag in the form of a competitor. Another ex-army captain, a peer of mine, has also set up a security company. A man with personal wealth, upper-class background, connections. Blah blah. That I can deal with.' Liam upturned his palms. 'I've got no issue with healthy competition but this guy plays dirty.

Now Liam's whole stance hardened, his jaw clenched and anger iced the cobalt of his eyes. But before he could speak the waiter returned and placed their dishes in front of them. Ava murmured thank you and waited for him to go before she looked expectantly at Liam.

'We are both in contention for a really important contract with Beaumont Industries and AJ Mason has orchestrated a smear campaign, designed to make me look vulnerable and weak.'

Ava stared at him and once again her hormones did a funny little flip. There wasn't even a hint of weakness or vulnerability in sight. The man was sheer power, from the craggy strength of his features to every sinew of his body. Compact lithe muscle, and now her eyes lingered on the breadth of his thigh, moved up to see the wall of his chest and the sculpted swell of his shoulders in the fine linen shirt. She blinked. *Get a grip.* What was wrong with her? Perhaps her starved hormones were so happy to have lighted on an attractive man they had decided to make hay whilst the sun shone. And who could blame them?

'The man sounds like a dirtbag. Surely you can get him for libel or slander or…something.'

'My problem is timing. My tender for the Beaumont contract needs to go in in a month. I don't have time to take AJ to court and, to be honest, even if I do it won't counterpunch the impact of all the online lies and the background venom. My reputation will be in shreds.'

'So where do I fit in?'

Liam looked down at his plate, pushed it away and topped up their glasses. 'I'm a widower.' His voice was flat, factual, and Ava kept her expression neutral, even as sympathy touched her. Liam could be little more than thirty; his wife must have been tragically young to die. There had been no mention of a wife on his company bio, no mention of a wife full stop in the Internet search she had conducted. 'My wife died five years ago. Since then I haven't had another relationship. AJ claims that I have never recovered from the tragedy and as time goes on it is affecting me more and more. So I need to *show* everyone that I am perfectly OK, on my game, my edge honed and nowhere near a nervous breakdown. I also need to counter his connections, his background and so on.'

'So what are you proposing? Exactly.' Ava remained still though every instinct told her not to wait for the answer but to push back her chair and run for it.

His gaze met hers full on; one deep breath and then he launched. 'I want you to pose as my girlfriend.'

It took all her social poise not to drop the sterling silver cutlery into her trout. Perhaps AJ Mason had a point. Perhaps Liam Rourke had lost the plot. But forget nervous breakdown—the man was bonkers. 'Excuse me?'

'I want you and I to fake a relationship.' The suggestion was uttered with a calm that quite simply did not gel with the sheer preposterousness of the idea. 'Unless of course you already have a partner? I did do some research of my own but I realise that may not have been sufficient.'

For a moment Ava considered simply making up a boyfriend, then dismissed the idea as craven. 'No. I am currently single.' Had been for the past four years. Since the Nick debacle, her one serious relationship.

Nick Abingworth had been a producer, met in the heady days of Ava's modelling career, and he was Hollywood handsome, charming and charismatic. Ava had fallen for the façade, believed it to front a good guy, a hero. Had harboured rose-tinted dreams of a happy ever after.

Had forgotten all the lessons learned from her parents' marriage. A marriage where Karen Casseveti's love for her husband had been an obsession. As for James, he'd loved Karen's wealth and connections, loved them so much he'd left his first family.

But Ava had forgotten all about the folly of one-sided love, disregarded the knowledge that love could be bought, faked with an eye to the main chance. Had believed she and Nick were different. Turned out she'd been wrong. When her dad had suffered his first heart attack and Ava had given up modelling to enter Dolci, had no longer been a celebrity party girl, Nick had shown his true colours and a swirl of dust as he'd legged it out of the door. Said he was sorry but she'd changed, was no longer the woman he'd fallen in love with. *Ciao.*

That had been that and, as far as Ava was concerned, that was how it would remain. 'Definitely single,' she added for emphasis. 'With no interest in a relationship. Of any type.'

'Think of it as a charade. A ruse to refute the idea that I haven't got over my wife.'

Have you? The question nearly fell from her lips and she bit it back. That was none of her business. Plus the man hadn't dated in five years—he didn't sound over it. But that was beside the point—the point was that this plan was granola nuts.

'It won't work. For a start, don't you think AJ will find the timing a wee bit suspect?'

'He might, but he can hardly suggest that I have persuaded or bribed Ava Casseveti to play along with a fake relationship. Why would you?'

'Well, there's an excellent question. Why would I?'

'Because you want to make amends for your father's actions. This is how you can do that. There's a certain poetic justice in the idea—a Casseveti *helping* a Rourke with a business plan.'

Touché. Ava closed her eyes as a swell of panic threatened. Every instinct told her this was not a good idea. Liam Rourke was too… much. Too good-looking, too attractive, and that was not what she needed right now. Her hormones were way too volatile around Liam. She could almost feel her carefully ordered world fraying at the edges. 'I see that, but this idea is… Well, it's pants. I mean, how would it even work?'

He shrugged. 'We fake a relationship, we go out for dinner, give some interviews, attend business functions together, get seen, generate some *positive* publicity for me. Right or wrong, people will be impressed by you, your position, your credentials.'

A stab of hurt pinged her ribs. Obviously all Liam Rourke wanted was the Ava Casseveti persona, the aristocrat, the celebrity model, the businesswoman. Not Ava herself. She gave her head a small shake at her own idiocy. Why would he want anything else? 'Actually, right now they may not be. The current public verdict on me is that I am a ditzy airhead who won't be able to keep her company from going under. A woman her own father didn't trust at the helm.' She met his gaze directly. 'So I may be a liability rather than an asset.'

For a moment he considered her words, his fingers drumming on the snow-white linen of the tablecloth. 'Nope. I don't think so. You are still my best option. This may even help you.'

'How?'

'It will distract people from a consideration of your business problems.'

'Hah! They'll think I'm fiddling whilst my desserts flambé.'

This pulled a smile from him. 'Not necessarily. If we publicise our relationship properly we can orchestrate some interviews that will give you a real chance to put your case forward.'

'It's too high risk.' Ava contemplated him, realised that Liam Rourke represented danger, high risk, high octane. Everything Ava Casseveti didn't do. 'It wouldn't work. We are strangers. Worse than strangers.' Her gaze met his. 'There is too much history between us. We are natural enemies. We couldn't pull this off.'

His lips twisted. 'Sounds to me like an excuse. This is all about our history. You told me two weeks ago you wanted to make amends on your father's behalf. This is how you can do it. Your choice.'

What to do? What to do?

Liam's words came back to her.

'Nothing can atone for that betrayal. His perfidy broke my father. He felt cheated and bitter, a bitterness that pervaded and corroded his life.'

But it was more than that—it would have corroded Liam's as well.

Conflict warred within her—the desire to do what was 'right' versus the instinct for self-preservation. But this wasn't about self, wasn't about Ava. The crux of the matter was the wrong done by her father and his desire to try to make it right. If she walked away now she would fail, would let her father down. And herself. In reality there was no choice. 'Fine. I'll do it. I'm in.'

Even as the words fell from her disbelief caused her to clasp her hands together under the table, to resist the urge to pinch herself in the hope she'd wake up.

'Excellent.' His low voice held satisfaction and appreciation and a funny little thrill shot through her as he raised his glass; his cobalt-blue eyes held hers and the shiver of anticipation and panic intensified. 'To us,' he said, just as their waiter shimmied towards the table, dessert menu in hand.

Instantly she raised her own glass and smiled, her best 'Ava Casseveti thinks you're great' smile. 'To us,' she echoed. Once the waiter had cleared their table and glided out of earshot she nodded. 'I understand now why you picked here for dinner. You're hoping that word will get to AJ that you were here with me.'

'Not only AJ. People in general. Some of my clients are ex-military or have military connections. It will all help.'

Ava looked down at the glossy card as her brain grappled to come to terms with what she had agreed to. 'Right now what will help is a melt-in-the-middle chocolate pudding and an espresso.'

Liam smiled, the effect electric. Ava felt her pulse rate ratchet, as warmth flooded her body, and she reached for her water glass. 'You're right.'

Whilst that was gratifying she only seemed able to focus on his smile. Her gaze snagged on the firm contour of his lips. *Enough.* 'I know. There isn't much in life that chocolate pudding can't help.'

Once the dessert arrived Ava tasted it experimentally. 'This is good. Not as good as Dolci's, of course.' His lips tightened imperceptibly and she wished the words back. Dolci was hardly the best topic to bring up. 'Sorry.'

He shook his head. 'Don't apologise. Obviously I can hardly expect you not to mention Dolci over the next three months.'

The chocolate melted to ash in her mouth and she dropped the spoon with a clank. 'Three months? Three weeks would be hard enough. Three months...is a quarter of a year.'

'We need the time or people will know it's fake.'

'But we can't sustain a lie of this magnitude for three months.'

'Surely it won't be so bad for you? You were a model. I assume you had to act, project, exaggerate feelings.'

'Yes. For *a photo shoot*, and I was projecting my love for perfume, or chocolate, not a real live person. For a very short space of time. For the benefit of the camera, not a live audience. *And* if I made a mistake I got another go.'

He raised a hand. 'I get it.'

'No. I really don't think you do. Besides, forget me.' After all, she'd spent her whole life playing the various personae of Ava Casseveti, perfect daughter, perfect girlfriend... celebrity...heiress, aristocrat. 'What about you? How are you going to pull it off?'

'That's my problem.'

'Nope. It is *our* problem. If we are exposed

we will both look like idiots. Both be publicly humiliated. *We* have to make this look real.'

There was a silence and then he nodded. 'Fair point.' He picked up his coffee cup. 'How about we meet tomorrow for a brainstorming session? Give us both some time to think about a strategy to make this work. Perhaps we could meet at Dolci headquarters? So I can get accustomed to the idea I am dating a Casseveti.'

Ava felt a small tug of surprise. Liam had listened to her, taken her comments on board. 'Works for me. I'll see you there.'

CHAPTER FOUR

LIAM STOOD OUTSIDE the offices of Dolci's headquarters the following evening and looked up at the impressive glass-fronted façade. Memory rocked him. His father had brought him here once and for a few tension-filled moments twelve-year-old Liam had believed that Terry Rourke would storm inside and cause an affray. Remembered anxiety echoed a hollow ring in his gut.

Now, nineteen years later, Terry was dead and Liam stood here on the brink of a fake relationship with Ava Casseveti. About to gain entrance into the enemy's portals. Would his father approve of this? Of course he would—he would appreciate that a Casseveti had been forced into a contract with a Rourke. And his mother. How would she feel?

Liam had no idea. His relationship with his mother was too distant for him to hazard a guess. He loved his mum, of course he did, but that love was layered with strands of guilt and knowledge of how his selfish behaviour had impacted on her happiness.

As a child he'd hero-worshipped his father, blamed his mother for the breakdown of his parents' marriage, hadn't understood how hard it was for her to watch Terry Rourke slowly but surely give his life over to the bottle. Lose his job, his dignity, his body and soul vanishing into a maudlin, alcoholic haze. Liam hadn't got Bea's struggle to try and keep a roof over their heads and food on the table. All Liam had wanted was for his father to get better and his parents to be happy again.

Then, when Liam was twelve, Bea had met someone else, a plumber at the hospital where she'd worked as a nurse—John Malone—and they'd fallen in love. She'd been full of joy, had planned to leave her husband, had expected Liam to understand, to go with her.

Liam had been horrified at having his illusory bubble burst, had refused point-blank to leave his dad, and in the end Bea had stayed in the marriage. For Liam's sake.

Guilt at his actions tugged but before he could contemplate further Ava walked through the revolving glass door and headed towards him. And dammit again, she stopped him in his tracks, derailed his senses for a smidgeon of time, dressed today in elegant tailored grey trousers topped by a black top and cinched at the waist with a wide belt. 'Hi.'

'Hi,' he managed and for that fleeting instant they both simply stood and then she stepped back. 'Come on up.'

Through a marbled lobby, walls decorated with glittering photographs of Casseveti success. James shaking hands with a renowned global businessman, Ava in a photo shoot to promote Dolci products… Liam absorbed it all, ensured he kept his stance relaxed during the trip in a state-of-the-art elevator, a walk through a now empty open-plan work area, dotted with desks and equipment and then they entered a spacious meeting room. A large oval glass-topped table graced the centre, a tray with coffee, tea and biscuits had been set out, a whiteboard was ready at the front. The perfect setting for a business brainstorming session.

Liam placed his briefcase on the table. 'I think the best way is to sit down and swap some basic facts, the sort of information that it would be natural for us to have.'

Ava sat down and opened a leather-bound folder. 'Agreed. I've prepared a CV but with some extra personal information. Like how I like my tea.'

'I did a fact sheet. Though I have to admit I didn't include my tea preference. Good call.' That was the exact detail they would be expected to know. 'I take mine strong with just a hint of milk.' Ava already had a pen in hand and was jotting the information down, and for a moment he caught a glimpse of the column of her neck as she bent over the table.

For an overlong instant his gaze was caught and a pang shot through him, one he damped down immediately. 'Let's read each other's information and then try and learn it. We can test each other later.'

She nodded agreement and pushed her CV across the table. He noted that her nails were a different colour from the previous day and for a moment he wondered how hard it must be to coordinate her outfits so well. Wondered if attention to nails would feature on her fact list.

He watched her as she studied his piece of paper, the small fierce crease of concentration, the way she pressed her lips together. Dammit, now he'd snagged on those lips his gaze lingered for a moment and he quickly turned his attention to the paper on the table. Started to commit the facts to memory: her birthday, names of her schools, private education, top grades, various dance awards, excellent university, and then her two-year stint in the modelling world.

Then she'd quit modelling and gone into the family firm, where she'd held roles in different departments until her father's death six months ago. Never owned a pet, enjoyed dancing, fashion and shoes. As he came to the end of the sheet he looked back up at her and caught her studying him.

'Right,' she said. 'I think I'm getting the facts. I know your birthday, where you were born and a bit about your family. Your mum is called Bea, your stepdad is called John and his son is called Max and he is fourteen.' She stopped and he was aware he'd flinched as more memories cascaded in.

Two years after Bea decided to stay with her husband, John had married someone else, and Liam could still remember his mother's grief when she'd found out. He'd seen the anguish in her grey eyes, heard the sound of muted tears in the night, seen her feet drag and heard her voice snap. It had only been then that he'd begun to understand what his mother had sacrificed for him and he hadn't known how to handle that.

So he'd renewed his efforts to make his dad better, make him reform, make his parents be happy again. To no avail. So in the end at eighteen he'd done what he'd thought was right. He'd joined the army. He'd known that once he had a new 'home' and independence his mother would be able to leave. Finally accepted too that his father was not going to change.

Then Bea had reconnected with John, by then divorced and the father of a three-year-old son, Max. Bea and John got married and Liam was happy for them. But he knew that he had thwarted their chance of an earlier life together, a chance to have children of their own. And that created an awkwardness and a discomfort and so he stayed clear as much as he could, wanted to allow his mum a second chance to have a happy family life.

But he'd put none of the detail on his fact sheet. All Ava needed were facts, not the grim story that shadowed them. Facts were important.

'That's right.'

Ava nodded. 'I've been thinking about this. Are you going to tell your mum the truth about us?'

'No. The fewer people who know, the better. The best way to keep a secret is to make sure it is a secret.'

'I get that but she is hardly going to be happy that her son is dating a Casseveti. I'll need to meet her during this charade and that will be awkward, to say the least. So why put her through it? Surely you can trust her to keep the secret?'

'It's not just my mum. It's John and Max as well. It doesn't seem fair to ask her to keep it secret from them. And Max is only fourteen. It seems even more unfair to ask him to keep a secret like that or to lie for us. I won't ask her or her family to do that.' Wouldn't complicate her life or upset her family dynamic in any way.

'That is a fair point. But—'

'It does make it extra hard on you. I'm sorry. I'll shield you as best I can when we meet her. And we'll keep it brief.' That would hardly be a surprise to any of them. Liam kept his visits short and polite. 'And whilst my mum will have some negative feelings, she knows you aren't to blame for your father's actions.'

Ava hesitated and then shrugged. 'OK. This is your show. Could you arrange for us to meet them once we have figured out our act properly. Before we go public?'

'Sure. And what about your mum?'

'We will have to tell my mother the truth. She knows who you are and about my father's request.'

'Will she keep it secret?'

'Yes. My mum is the Queen of Spin. She will see that our relationship can be spun to Dolci's advantage. She won't mess with that.' Ava gave a decisive nod and glanced down at her printed agenda, then up at her computer screen, tucked a stray tendril of hair behind her ear. This must be exactly how she looked in a business meeting.

She looked up. 'Right, next on the agenda— we need to get our story straight. Get our facts lined up in a row.'

She rose to her feet and headed towards the whiteboard. 'I thought we could plot out a timeline, work out some plot points. Then I'll type it up.'

'Sure. Good plan.' And it was…yet something wasn't right with the current scenario. Sure, they now knew more about each other but…

Moving along a few seats, he watched the unconscious grace with which she moved. As she reached for the pen, again her nail colour caught his eye, the pale pink a perfect complement to the grey of her suit, the crisp businesslike white of her shirt. Her lips a perfect match. Liam frowned, tried to home in on what his instinct was trying to tell him.

Knew it was not that he had a nail fetish.

'Right,' Ava said. 'I've thought about this and it's really important we figure out when our "relationship"— she made quote marks in the air —started. The times have to add up and stand up to scrutiny. We can't say we were having a romantic dinner at The Ritz if that's the day they were closed for renovations.'

'Agreed.'

'Good. So…' She broke off. 'Are you listening?' she asked.

'Yes, I am, and you're right. All that is important but…' He hesitated. 'We're doing this all wrong.'

'I don't understand.'

He wasn't sure he did either, but he trusted his instincts and this was too important to ignore them. 'You are right to say that this will only work if we can pull it off, and to do that we need all these facts. But this isn't the way to collate them.'

'Why not?'

He started to pace. 'Because this is how we'd conduct a work meeting. And whilst this is a business arrangement, the fake relationship isn't a business one. If we spend hours in a boardroom we may come up with a good theoretical plan and a list of facts about each other but that won't help us be authentic. Because there's lots of information that we won't have included. For example, you didn't mention how much effort you put into your appearance. It must take time to change the colour of your nails on such a regular basis.'

Ava frowned. 'It didn't even occur to me to mention my nails.'

'Exactly. That's the sort of thing that takes time and being together for real.'

'But are my nails really that important?'

'I don't know. But I do know if you send an undercover agent in somewhere you send someone who knows the territory, understands the language and the community. I don't know about you but I haven't been in a relationship for a long time. It's unfamiliar terrain.' And one he'd completely destroyed in his marriage.

'So you think we need some hands-on practice rather than studying the theory.' Her eyes widened and heat crept up her cheekbones. 'That came out all wrong. I didn't mean literal hands-on practice...' She raised her hands to touch her cheeks. 'Now I am making this worse.'

He couldn't help the smile that tugged his lips, even as desire sparked in his gut. 'I know what you meant. We can come up with the best story in the world, learn all these facts, but a play is only as good as the actors.'

'And we aren't actors.'

'Exactly, so we have to maximise our chances of managing to fake this. I think we need to get more…comfortable round each other, and that means spending time together outside a boardroom.'

'So what do you suggest?'

'Let's go on a date. Right now. A trip on the London Eye. We provided security at an event there recently and we were given a season pass for Rourke Securities employees. I'm pretty sure I can get us an upgrade. We can discuss a timeline, whilst looking out over London in a private pod.'

'Isn't it a bit risky? I don't think we are exactly ready to launch.'

'I get that.' Liam shrugged. 'But it's not as though we need to speak to anyone or give an interview. It will give us "relationship experience" and add evidence to our dating history.'

'Agreed.'

'Give me five minutes to make a couple of calls.'

Fifteen minutes later they were on their way, in the back of a chauffeur-driven car. Ava glanced sideways at him, ridiculously aware of his proximity. She'd watched him as he'd made this happen, the mix of crisp efficiency and charm that had secured them the private pod, and his sheer dynamism had sparked a frisson. Now her hormones were having difficulties mastering the concept of a fake date. But she had them on a tight leash, was sat squashed against the window, as far from him as it was possible to be. Hell, if anyone opened the door she'd tumble out. And Liam was no better. Yet the idea of moving across seemed way too fraught and relief swathed through her as the car glided to a stop.

They climbed out to walk the remainder of the way, the cool London evening breeze a welcome hit as they made their way towards the huge lit-up wheel. She tried to walk a little closer to him to get in character as their breath wisped white on the brisk February air.

Once there, a friendly member of staff approached and conferred with Liam, who then turned to Ava. 'Usually the pod comes with a host. Are you happy to sign a waiver to say you're OK without one?'

'Of course.' Minutes later they were standing in the pod, glass of champagne in hand.

'Are they really OK letting us on without a host?'

'Sure. I've said that we'll treat it as a test of their security and health and safety measures. Lots of people would rather not have a host so we're testing it for them. Last thing we need is to be observed close up.'

'Definitely not.' Ava looked out over the London night sky as the wheel began to move, so slowly it felt almost like magic, as if they were lifted by gossamer threads. 'It's beautiful by night. I came here in the day with a couple of colleagues once but this is completely different. All the landmarks look like a fairy tale.' Come to that, this all felt like a fairy tale. And it had nothing to do with the lights or the champagne and everything to do with Liam's presence. He was right. This was completely different from the boardroom, but she still wasn't at all sure it was in a good way. Or perhaps it was too good. Because here if she moved ever so slightly she'd be right next to him, would be able to feel the solid press of his muscular thigh against her leg, would be able to inhale the tang of expensive soap, study the way his hair curled over his ear and…

Time to talk, time to find poised, aristocratic, socially adept Ava, and she wrenched her gaze to the London landscape. 'It's amazing, really—I mean, who designed it? A glorified Ferris wheel that has become one of the main tourist attractions in London.'

'It was built by a husband and wife team.

And it's about one hundred and thirty-five metres tall with a diameter of one hundred and twenty metres. The pods weigh ten tonnes and—' Five minutes later he broke off and ran a hand over the back of his neck. 'Jeez. Sorry. I didn't even know I *knew* all of that.'

'That's OK.' She was pretty sure Liam was as on edge as she was. 'You made all those facts interesting.' Seeing his eyebrows rise in clear disbelief, she smiled. 'Honestly. You did. You'd make a great tour guide.'

He gave a mock groan. 'And a terrible date.'

'Nope.' She shook her head. 'Actually…it's kind of sweet.'

'Sweet?' His tone mixed incredulity and distaste and she laughed.

'Yup. And it proves your point. Being here made those facts personal…and that is the best way to get to know each other. But it's also a bit…strange. Because it's a date that's not a date.'

'And we aren't natural around each other.' He took a deep breath. 'Yet.'

'Maybe it will just take time. A few more dates like this. Sitting in a car together…'

'And not squashing ourselves up against the doors,' he said and now they smiled at each other.

'Exactly. Maybe a week or so—we could walk round parks, hang out…get a bit more used to each other. I mean, we barely know each other, and our history makes it even more complicated. It's hard to base a relationship on—' She broke off as instinct prickled the back of her neck.

'What's wrong?'

'Nothing. Just keep talking. But I think we've been spotted.' Out of the corner of her peripheral vision, she saw someone point at their pod, camera in hand. 'We *have* been spotted.' Her mind went into overdrive; on automatic she appraised the scene. Champagne, private pod, the whole thing shrieked of date night. This was the perfect set-up for a launch of their relationship; discovered by accident, it would reek of authenticity.

Instinct took over and, leaning over, she kissed him. Her intent had been a simple, quick, featherlight brush of the lips but she hadn't bargained for her body's reaction. Or his. Because it wasn't enough—the sheer giddy sensation whirled her head. After a first startled second where he froze, he turned his body, raised his hands and cupped her face; the firm, cool grasp made her catch her breath.

Then he deepened the kiss, slowly, lan-

guorously, as if they had all the time in the
world, and Ava forgot where she was, forgot
everything except this heady moment in time
where nothing mattered except the sweet sensations that glided through her whole body.
Then all too soon it was over, the wheel literally stopped turning and Ava realised they
were near the top.

As she pulled away she caught sight of his
expression, knew it mirrored her own. Shell
shock, surprise. *All wrong,* screamed the one
bit of her brain that was still in gear. *Pull this
together.* Seamlessly she pulled a smile to her
lips and whispered, 'Don't look surprised.'
Knew that a photo like that splashed on social media would give away too much.

To her relief Liam got it instantly, leant forward to hide his expression, looked as though
he were whispering sweet nothings in her ear,
and then he moved away to pick up the champagne bottle to top up their glasses, a smile
of sorts on his lips.

Ava focused on breathing, sipped the champagne, wished it were the bubbles that were
swirling her head rather than the aftermath of
the kiss. 'Sorry. I reacted on instinct—I saw
an opportunity to make this look real and I
took it without thinking.'

'There's no need to apologise—you took

me by surprise, that's all.' With an obvious effort he cleared his throat, brought his voice to a normal tone. 'What do you think will happen now?'

Ava shrugged. 'It's hard to know. It could be absolutely nothing, it could be the photo goes viral on social media. My feeling is it will land somewhere in between. There will be a buzz of interest because of who I am and it may or may not pick up.'

Liam rubbed the back of his neck, gave her a rueful smile. 'Sorry. You were right earlier. This was a bad idea. If interest is piqued we aren't ready yet.'

'No.' But it was impossible to feel irritation with a man who was willing to admit fault.

'Hmm…' She could almost see his brain go into overdrive. 'I've got an idea. Let's go back to my place—I need to make some calls.'

Forty-five minutes later the car came to a smooth stop and the driver opened the door. Ava smiled her thanks as she climbed out and looked around her at the large Edwardian London house.

She followed him through the front door and down a spacious hallway. "The lounge is through here. Drink?' he asked.

'A cup of tea would be perfect.'

'Coming up. Milk, one sugar, right?'

'Right.'

He left the room and she took the opportunity to look around. The room was functional and comfortable with clean lines and colours. Yet it could be a show room—there were no photographs or anything out of place or cluttered. Sitting down on a luxuriously comfortable arm chair she wondered where Liam was. Perhaps the kitchen was miles away or the kettle had broken or he'd run out of tea bags.

On that thought the door opened and he reappeared. 'Tea and biscuits.'

'Perfect.' He sat opposite her and she raised her eyebrows. 'You look pleased with yourself.'

'I am. I've figured out a solution to our need-to-get-to-know-each-other-fast problem.'

'Go ahead.' Ava eyed him and a sudden premonition tickled the back of her neck, told her that his next words were going to be humdingers.

'A mini break in Italy.'

'Mini break? Italy?' Parrot, anyone?

'Yes. Sometimes I have clients who need to meet away from the public eye. If two businesses are planning a merger and want to keep it under the radar they want privacy and security. I provide that—Rourke Security has a number of discreet, secure, safe locations. We can use one of those and spend the weekend there.

'Um…'

'It's a little village in Puglia. It's beautiful and a tourist attraction so we can blend in as simple tourists. It's a low-key way to practise being a couple. I've got a flight sorted out for tomorrow evening and I've spoken to Elena, the housekeeper there. She'll have it all ready and—'

'Whoa.' Was he for real? 'Hang on a sec. You've done all that? I haven't even agreed—you haven't even asked my opinion.'

'That's what I'm doing now.'

'No. Actually it isn't. You've arranged everything. Sounds like it's a done deal.' It all felt like shades of her whole life, other people in control, deciding her actions and her future. Pleasing her father, her mother, Nick… Ever since she was a child she'd done what she was supposed to, done the right thing, worked so very hard to be the perfect daughter. She'd worn the clothes her mother bought her, taken dance exams, played the violin. To please her father she'd studied hard, made the right friends, walked the path her parents sent her down. Jumped when she was told to jump. Because she had always known she was the glue that bound the Casseveti family.

Now this man had done the same, made decisions for her and suddenly Ava was furious.

Liam sighed. 'There would be no point wasting time in a consultation if I couldn't deliver.'

'Well, how do you know *I* could deliver? You don't know me—I could be afraid of flying. I could be allergic to Italy. I may not want to spend the whole weekend with you in a strange place. Or anywhere, for that matter. *I* may have had some ideas.'

A pause and then Liam held up his hand. 'You're right. I sprang it on you as a fait accompli.' Now he shook his head. 'Discussion was never my strong point.' The words were muttered under his breath and she was sure she wasn't meant to hear them. 'I apologise.'

Ava blinked; she could practically feel the moral high ground drop from under her feet.

Then he smiled, a small quick smile, and she could feel her ire start to lose its heat. 'So let's start again,' he said. 'Are you scared of flying?'

Ava looked at him. 'No. I was speaking hypothetically.' Plus as a model she had done photo shoots all over the world—Liam had been well within his rights to assume air travel wasn't an issue.

His gaze met hers. 'Any allergies?'

Now Ava sighed and saw his lips quiver ever so slightly in clear amusement and her eyes narrowed.

'Perhaps an allergy to pizza. Pasta, spaghetti or lasagne.' He put on an Italian accent and now Ava couldn't help it—her own lips turned up in a reluctant grin.

'Ha ha! OK. You got me. No allergies.'

'Then on to your next point. Here you are completely correct—I should never have assumed you would feel safe coming to Italy to spend a weekend with a stranger. If it makes you feel better I have a housekeeper there who can stay in the house—Elena is a lovely woman.'

'Thank you. I appreciate all of that. But it wasn't my physical safety I was thinking about. It just feels a bit intense to spend a whole weekend together. A bit daunting.'

'Agreed,' he said.

The word gave her a sudden hard kick of reality. If this was hard for her it would be doubly so for Liam. The last woman he would have gone on a mini break with was his wife. This whole charade must be incredibly hard for him on so many levels, which prompted the question: 'Are *you* sure you want to do this?'

'I'm sure. I won't let AJ Mason get away with this. He will not take my company and my reputation away from me. I won't let that happen. Or at least not without a fight.'

Ava had to respect that determination, had to concede as well that the idea had merits.

They would be tucked away out of the public eye and it would give them much-needed time to get comfortable around each other and practise their roles.

'Then, Italy, here we come.'

CHAPTER FIVE

THE FOLLOWING DAY as they approached the airfield Ava tried to quell the butterflies that flitted around her tummy in a maelstrom of panic. She sneaked a sideways glance at Liam. His gaze was focused on the road and there was no indication of any nerves in his demeanour. For a moment her gaze touched on the firm line of his jaw, the sweep of his nose and the surprising length of his dark eyelashes. For one stupid moment she wondered what it would be like if this were real, and a little shiver ran through her body.

All in all it was a relief to arrive at the airfield. 'So this is your plane?' she asked as they approached the craft.

'It belongs to Rourke Securities. A client has asked for an item to be delivered privately in Europe. My pilot will drop us off en route.'

Soon after, the plane started its ascent and Ava looked around the compact but comfortable area, complete with a small table and soft leather reclining chairs.

In the interest of showing that she was back in control of her nerves she put on her best social expression. 'So do you own a lot of planes?'

Liam shook his head. 'Just this one. Sometimes I have clients who want to broker a deal and they figure high up in the air is the best place to do it. Sometimes I have to move a team of people fast and safely and discreetly. Or move cargo. I do try to combine assignments where I can to limit the ecological impact. I need this plane to run my business but I minimise airmiles. If I can transport by land or even sea I do. And the company does support a number of environmental charities.'

Surprise touched her. 'I didn't have you down as someone who would care about the environment.'

'I think we all have to. Don't get me wrong, I'm not giving up air travel, but I figure every little counts.'

'I agree and I'd really like Dolci to do more. I'd like to use more local suppliers and really look at how much unnecessary plastic we use. Analyse how we can minimise impact to the environment.'

'Then do it.'

He made it all sound so simple, as if she could wave a magic wand. 'It's not that easy.'

'Why not?'

The slight quirk in his voice goaded her, as if she were all talk and no skirt. 'For a start I am not in sole charge. My half-siblings have equal shares.'

'According to press reports they aren't exactly showing up to work—maybe they wouldn't object? Have you asked them?'

Ava pressed her lips together—her 'family' problems weren't to be shared. 'No. They'd probably lawyer up.' Or simply stonewall her. At the moment Luca Petrovelli would only communicate through lawyers and his standard response was that he couldn't give an opinion until he came to an agreement with his sister. As for Jodi, she didn't respond at all, after her initial reply that simply said to refer to her brother. Frustration gnawed Ava's insides and tensed her muscles and she forced her body to relax. 'But I did ask my father and he was less than keen. He wanted to do the minimum needed to "look good", believed profit trumped ethics.' Even an appeal to his conscience hadn't worked. He'd listened to her ideas and then he'd vetoed them. Instead he had donated privately to an environmental charity.

'You don't still have to do as your father wanted. This is something you clearly feel passionate about. So own it. Make Dolci a forerunner on the environment.'

'It doesn't feel right. Dolci was built on the foundations of my dad's ethos, his drive, his ideas and beliefs. And they worked. I don't want to go against his wishes and I'd probably be a fool to do so.'

'But times change and people change. Your father had his vision, now it's time for yours.'

'Just like that?' Her whole life had been spent being the perfect daughter, following her parent's wishes, or at least ensuring they coincided with her own—she wasn't sure she knew how to stop. 'Dolci is his legacy. I can't trample over that. My vision may send Dolci down the pan. Then that would be my responsibility. My fault.' Because she wasn't good enough, wasn't perfect and would finally be exposed in all her lack of glory. The idea shivered panic-stricken fear through her and she clenched her nails into her palms. Sparked determination—Dolci would not go under, not on her watch. 'And that isn't going to happen.' She shook her head. 'Anyway, right now we need to be talking about our fake relationship and how to make it believable.' In truth she had no idea how this conversation had gone so off-piste.

Liam waited a heartbeat and for a second she thought he'd demur, pursue the topic of Dolci. Then, 'You're right. Where should we start?'

'It's all about the detail. The only way to spin a fabrication is to make sure it stands up to scrutiny.' A rule she'd learnt in the cradle or possibly even the womb. After all, Karen had spun the Casseveti story into a fairy tale and that had been no easy task. Somehow she'd managed to completely gloss over James leaving his first family and painted instead the magical romance of a lifetime between the Lady and the entrepreneur. Compared to that this should be a walk in the park. 'Let's start with our first meeting.'

'Three months ago you consulted me on a security issue. Maybe you were worried about industrial sabotage. That makes sense. After your father's death that would be a legitimate worry, a good time for someone to strike. Then let's say a few weeks later, when you were no longer my client, I asked you out.'

'I wouldn't even have considered dating that close to his death. I was too caught up in grief.' The soul-shaking realisation that her father was gone for ever combined with the ramifications of his will.

'It doesn't work like that. There is something about death that makes the living clutch at life, affirm it, want to live it.' The depth of his voice told her that he spoke from experience and yet she shook her head in refutation.

'I wouldn't have, couldn't have agreed to a date just a few months later.'

'I met Jess when my dad was dying—we got married a few weeks after his funeral.' Impossible to tell what emotions underpinned his factual tone, but his blue eyes shadowed and clouded, reminded her of how much he had lost.

'I can't imagine how difficult, how complicated that must have been for you both. But I am glad that you did have Jess, that you had support and love and comfort.'

'Yes.' The harshness of his voice shocked her and she saw the shadow cross his face and ravage it. 'My point is that it is possible to start a relationship even when you are grieving.'

'Accepted.' She gestured with her hand, then did a quick calculation. 'So our first date would have been about two months ago. Where did we go for dinner?'

'Does it matter? Any random restaurant.'

His voice held impatience, perhaps a left-over from the emotions this conversation must have awoken, but she knew she couldn't let that go. 'It does matter and that really wouldn't work. One of the stock questions we'll be asked is where was our first date? We'll look a bit idiotic if we say it was at a "random restaurant".'

'OK.' But she could tell he still thought she was overreacting. 'Where did we go?'

Ava looked at him between narrowed eye-lids. 'That's up to you. Where would you have taken me on a first date? If this were real. Really real.' In the silence that followed she sensed the atmosphere shift. Pictured the meeting in his office, the dawn of attraction, the moment he asked her. 'Would you have called me? Emailed me? Where would you have taken me?' This was becoming too real and she needed to move, to walk, to leave this illusion. 'I'll pop to the bathroom whilst you come up with an answer.'

Liam watched Ava walk away, knew he only had a few minutes to conjure up a scenario for a hypothetical first date. *Chill.* He was CEO of a multinational company. He'd been in the army for eight years. How hard could this be?

All he had to do was pick a restaurant—an impressive restaurant, not a random one.

He'd narrowed it down to a shortlist by the time she returned. He held out the phone. 'Take your pick. London's most exclusive restaurants.'

She glanced down and shook her head. 'It won't work. How come no one spotted us? Given someone spotted us on the London Eye. Plus would you really have taken me to a glitzy restaurant when I was grieving?'

Liam sighed. 'No. You're right.'

'It's all in the detail. That's what makes a story feel authentic. That's why you have to really think about it.'

Problem was he didn't want to think about it, didn't want to imagine what it would be like to take Ava on a real first date, a date where the attraction was allowed, in the open, a date where they could flirt and banter and encourage the spark of attraction to ignite into a flare. Because even now Liam could sense the bubbling undercurrent of awareness that seethed between them, urged and tempted, beckoned him to…to where? Nowhere he wanted to go. Liam pressed his lips together. This was a purely hypothetical situation, a business exercise, no different from a military campaign or a security detail for a client.

'If we couldn't go to a restaurant maybe I'd have cooked you a meal. With candles.' That flickered and glinted and highlighted the corn colour of her hair. The strum of music in the background, a chilled bottle of wine on the table. Fresh flowers as a centrepiece. Her hand brushing his as pulled out her chair. Discomfort edged his gut at the sheer realness of the image and it was an effort not to squirm on the aircraft seat. After all, the last woman he had cooked dinner for had been Jess and he'd never felt like this, however hard he'd tried, and he had tried. Had convinced himself that the love would grow, that he could make himself love her. But every 'romantic' dinner had been a construct, an attempt to make something out of nothing. And all the candles had illuminated were the awkwardness and falsity.

Pulling himself to the present, he looked at Ava. 'Would that work?'

'I'm not sure. It doesn't ring true. Would you really ask someone to your house on a first date?' She leaned forward, placed a hand on his arm. 'This is hard for you, isn't it?' Ava said gently. 'I'm sorry. If you haven't dated since Jess this must bring back memories.'

'I'm fine,' he said. 'Give me a minute.' This was important—this was the way to defeat AJ Mason, salvage his reputation and win the Beaumont contract. Liam forced his brain into gear. 'How does this sound? A moonlit picnic in Hyde Park. A thick tweed picnic blanket, a hamper from an exclusive emporium, chilled white wine in crystal flutes all under the stars. We sat and talked and looked at the stars and discussed constellations and...'

'It was magical,' she said softly.

And for a moment it was; he was there. Could see himself laying the blanket on the grass. Could see them eating, feeding each other bits of food, then lying back and gazing up at the stars, side by side, so close that a tendril of her corn-blonde hair tickled his cheek.

There was a silence and now their gazes meshed and, dammit, instead of the neutral air of the cabin he could feel the fresh evening breeze, smell the scent of evening flowers almost taste the food. 'Detail is important,' he said. Aware of the husk in his voice.

'Yes.'

Did we kiss? The words so nearly fell from his lips and he swallowed them down just as Ava gave a small shaky laugh.

'Actually detail is important and that scenario won't work. Because two months ago it would have been December.'

Liam groaned. 'Dammit. I thought I had it down perfectly.'

'You did.' Her voice was soft. 'But it's back to the drawing board.'

'Not for long.' To his own consternation he already had the exact answer, his mind inexplicably now fizzing with dating ideas. 'This is it.'

'Go ahead.' Her eyes were wide now, her lips slightly parted.

'I would take you in a horse-drawn carriage through the park. We'd have a cosy blanket and sit side by side. There would be mince pies and mulled wine and we'd hear the clip clop of the horses' hooves…'

'And the jingle of the sleigh bells and smell the tang of snow in the air and watch the winter scenery go by whilst we talked and…'

Did we kiss? Again he swallowed the words, saying instead, 'Does that work?'

'Yes.' Why did he have the feeling Ava had answered his unspoken question? *Enough. Stop.* Relief swept through him as the pilot's voice came over the Tannoy. 'We'll be landing in ten, Liam.'

* * *

Ava's head whirled as they disembarked from the plane and it had nothing to do with the dusky Italian breeze and everything to do with whatever the hell had just happened. For a moment she'd been sure he'd kiss her; hell, for a moment she'd wanted him to kiss her. Had been so caught up in the imaginary magical moment that a real spell had been cast.

The breeze was welcome, and with any luck it would blow her mind back to order. Liam headed towards a car. 'Pierre is going to give us a lift. He is Elena the housekeeper's husband.'

The idea of a chaperone allowed her to gather a polite, friendly persona together for the ten-minute journey. As she chatted to the middle-aged flamboyant Frenchman the tension seeped from her shoulders.

'I miss my country,' the grizzled man said. 'But I know my Elena could not move from her home, her family, this beautiful place, and so I have adapted. That is the power of love.'

His declaration brought a smile to her face even as she marvelled at them. A sudden pang of envy touched her for what this man and his wife had. Even as she knew it wasn't for her. She did believe in the power of love and she'd seen how destructive that power could be. Seen her mother's love for her father send her to the verge of brittle breakdown. Karen Casseveti's whole life had been defined by her love to the exclusion of all else. Her fear of losing her husband had dictated her every move, even down to the decision to have a baby. And once she had Ava she had seen her as an asset in her quest. As Ava had grown up she had seen the fear in her mother's perfectly made-up eyes as her gaze tracked her husband across a room.

A justified fear because she had known how precarious her position was. Known that James had loved his first family and yet that love too had been destroyed, defeated by the power of ambition and the lure of wealth. James had needed Lady Karen Hales's money and connections to start Dolci and so he'd deserted his first wife and family.

So, yes, love was definitely a powerful force, but like any force it could cause pain.

The car glided to a stop and Ava blinked back to the present as she took in her surroundings. The whitewashed stone-walled building took picturesque to new levels of meaning. Iron balconies fronted the first floor and pretty trees lined the pavement outside.

Inside the rustic wood-panelled front door an elegant grey-haired woman bustled towards them, a welcoming smile on her face. *'Buona sera*, Liam. It is good to see you again.'

Liam stooped to kiss the woman on both cheeks. 'You too, Elena. How are the children? How is the latest addition?' He turned to Ava. 'Elena welcomed her fourth grandchild into the world two months ago.'

Ava smiled and stepped forward. 'Congratulations. I'm Ava.'

'Welcome, Ava. And thank you. Arianna is gorgeous, my first granddaughter and she is beautiful. Now to business. I have prepared food, done the shopping and stocked the bar and freezer. The beds are made up. If there is anything you need, call me. Or Pierre.' She smiled at Ava. 'This is my number. Please feel free to contact me as well. I live nearby. I can come any time.'

'Thank you, Elena. I'll input that now.'

'Then I will leave you to it. Unless you wish for me to wait and serve the food.'

'No need.' Liam paused and looked across at Ava. 'Unless you would prefer it.'

For a craven moment she wanted to say yes, didn't want to be left alone with Liam in this cosy, intimate setting to share a meal, just the two of them. *Ridiculous.* This was a working dinner and she and Liam had a lot of ground to cover and the whole *point* was for them to get comfortable around each other. *Alone*.

'No, I'm good, and thank you, Elena. The food smells incredible.'

Now Elena beamed. 'Thank you. I have made *focaccia barese* and *orecchiette con cime di rapa*. And a salad to accompany it. The dessert is my speciality—I will let that be a surprise. I will bring fresh breakfast pastries and bread in the morning.'

With that Elena left and Ava forced a smile to her face. 'So,' she said brightly. 'If it's OK with you I'll freshen up and unpack and then we can reconvene our discussion.'

'Sounds good.' He pointed. 'The kitchen is through there. I'll meet you down here in half an hour.'

Thirty minutes of reprieve and she needed every single one.

CHAPTER SIX

LIAM GAVE THE pasta a quick stir and lifted the lid to check on the simmering pan that emitted a waft of herbs with a hint of garlic. Anticipation clashed again with guilt and he reminded himself again that this was not a date. It was a working dinner.

The kitchen door opened and he looked up and there it was again, that little kick to his gut when he saw Ava. She'd changed into black trousers and a tunic top, her hair now pulled up into a bun. A kind of smart-casual-cum-business look. Her face looked a little different and he frowned as he tried to pinpoint it—perhaps a different lipstick and something about her eyes. Maybe a touch more eye shadow.

In the same moment he realised he was staring he also clocked that so was she, that her amber eyes watched him with…appreciation.

'Do I pass muster?' she asked.

'Yes. Do I?' he countered.

'Yes. Sorry to stare. There is just something great about a man at the kitchen stove. I know it's considered normal nowadays but in my family it wasn't.'

'I'd love to say I cooked it but you know I didn't. There is a bottle of wine in the fridge if you'd like a glass.'

'Thank you. I would. But I'll set the table first.'

'Great. The cutlery is in that drawer.'

The drawer that was right next to him, in a kitchen space that could best be described as cosy. Now what? If he moved away too abruptly it would look awkward. If he stayed put things could get even more awkward. Jeez. He was behaving like an adolescent. The whole point of this was so that they could get more comfortable together. Yet he could feel his body tense, brace itself for impact as Ava came closer. He could smell the scent of soap, a hint of elusive light floral scent. And now she was closer still and his muscles ached with tension when he heard her sudden intake of breath and knew his proximity affected her. The reminder that this attraction was mutual ratcheted his pulse rate.

'I...um... I...' She stood stock-still and he could see her gaze flick over him. Her hand lifted as if she were going to place it on his chest and then she dropped it quickly, masked the movement into a reach across to the drawer. He tried to move away and inadvertently his hand brushed against hers, his fingers swept over her wrist and she made the smallest of noises.

She leapt away as he did and somehow stepped back straight into him, her back pressed against his chest and he instinctively wrapped his arm around her waist to steady her and himself. And for one glorious second she pressed against him and all he wanted was to hold her and nuzzle kisses on the tantalising allure of her neck, to bury his face in the glossy, silken strands of her hair.

The instant vanished. He released her immediately and she sprang forward. 'Sorry,' they both said, their voices vying for supremacy.

Ava busied herself at the drawer, snatched up what looked like a random selection of cutlery and moved at pace towards the table, her back to him, whilst he dished up the food.

Eventually she cleared her throat and turned to face him, and for a moment there was silence as their gazes locked. 'So,' he managed. 'Do you cook?' It was the best he could do.

'Yes.' The assertion was over-emphatic, as if it characterised her relief that he'd initiated conversation. 'My mum insisted on me doing extensive cordon bleu courses. She believed a woman should be able to cook for her man.'

'You don't sound as if you agreed with her.'

'I didn't have a problem with learning a necessary skill—I just didn't understand why my dad never had to cook just because he didn't want to, but I had to learn how to make a soufflé when I didn't like it. To be fair I suppose Mum did a lot of the cooking as well.'

'I always imagined your family as having an array of staff, a butler and a cook and—' He broke off, knew the words were a mistake even as he said them.

'Did you imagine my family a lot?' Her voice held no judgement or censure yet the question irked him.

'Yes. I did. It was hard not to. In my father's mind your life of huge privilege should have been ours and he tended to dwell on it. His imagination fed by the numerous articles depicting the glittering life and times of the Cassevetis. It felt as if your success had a direct inverse correlation to my family's decline.' He knew his tone was bitter but right now he didn't care. 'Whilst you were learning how to bake a soufflé I was learning how to make nutritious meals on a shoestring. Meals that my dad would eat to soak up the booze. If I didn't cook he wouldn't eat.' *Whoa. Let's not turn this into a pity party.* And yet…it rankled. The realisation that whilst Karen Casseveti was cooking for her man his mum was working more and more extra shifts to try to pay the bills.

'I'm sorry.' Ava's voice was small but clear. There was compassion in her amber eyes and he didn't want that. It was too close to pity and his dad would have hated that from a Casseveti.

'There is no need for you to be sorry. You didn't do anything.'

Ava hesitated, ate a mouthful of the pasta and then looked at him. 'No, I didn't. But my father did. His actions were the catalyst that drove your father to alcohol.'

Innate honesty compelled Liam to point out, 'No one forced the whisky bottle to my dad's lips.' He did know that, would never understand why that was the choice his father had made. Had vowed it would never be his—he would always stand and fight. In Terry Rourke's place he would have taken the fight to the Cassevetis, proved himself to be the better man. 'That was his choice.'

'A choice that impacted on you and your mum.'

There was that compassion again and he wanted none of it. Neither would he brook

any criticism of his father however implicit.
Liam had loved his dad and known, for all
his faults, Terry had loved him too. 'Yes, it
did, but looking after my dad helped me too.
Kept me off the streets. I got a Saturday job
so I could get him vitamins.' All in his quest
to try to get his dad better, back to normal,
so that his parents could reunite, so that his
father would become the man he had once
been. 'The shop owner was in the army reserves and that got me interested in the army.
You don't need to be sorry for me.'

'I'm not. But I am sorry for my father's actions. More to the point, so was he.'

'Perhaps.'

'What do you mean "perhaps"?' Now anger
sharpened her tone. 'He asked me to come
and make amends. He regretted his actions.'

'But not enough to apologise in person, to
contact my dad or to meet me face to face.
Or pick up the phone himself. Over all the
years.' His anger matched hers now. Say what
she would, James Casseveti had been a coward and a cheat.

'My father found it hard to face his past.
I think he tried to block it out. Seeing you
would have evoked memories he didn't want
to think about.' Now her voice was sad. 'So
he decided to make amends for his wrongs

after he was gone—that way he wouldn't have to face the consequences himself.' Liam saw the confusion, the resignation that shadowed her face and he realised that now it was Ava who had to do just that. Ava who was left at the helm of Dolci, undermined by her father's shock decision to leave two thirds of her legacy to his first two children. Children who the press alleged he had deserted in their childhood. Ava who was faking a relationship. Anger with James combined with a sharp and unexpected desire to offer comfort.

What the heck? This was a Casseveti.

Ava pushed her empty plate to one side, leant forward, reached a hand out and then pulled it back. 'I know my dad was far from perfect and I know he did wrong. But he was my dad and I loved him.'

Hell. Those were words that could have fallen from his own lips.

'But I do believe he felt genuine regret. I wish…'

'That you could ask him. Talk to him.' He could see the grief in her eyes, recognised the shell-shock look of the finality of loss, the creeping realisation that the person was gone. The meaning of for ever took on new dimensions. And suddenly his anger disappeared. Ava had lost her father. However flawed he had been Ava had loved him. Just as Liam had loved his own dad. James Casseveti had done wrong but Ava hadn't and it was time to lay the past to rest. In order to make this work, but also because that was the right thing to do.

'Yes.' For a second her voice registered surprise and then understanding dawned in her amber eyes. 'You understand because you've been through it. Does it get easier? All I want is to somehow bring him back and ask him what I should do. Why he did some of the things he did.'

'I used to go Dad's grave. I'd sit there and ask him questions, try to imagine the answers. It gave me a level of peace. Still does sometimes.' Surprise touched him that he was sharing this, but how could he ignore a grief he recognised all too well? 'Although he's gone he is still part of you. For better or worse he helped shape your life. Nothing can change that or erase the good memories. As for the grief, it doesn't go but it compacts, becomes a small part of you that you carry, a mark of respect and love for the person who is gone.' He rubbed the back of his neck to mitigate the prickle of embarrassment. 'That's my two pennyworth.'

'It's worth a lot more than that.' He looked

across and saw that tears glistened in her beautiful amber eyes. 'That has helped more than you can know. It's been hard—I don't have any siblings, or at least not any who will share this grief. My mother is devastated so it feels wrong to burden her. So thank you—it means a lot to talk to someone who gets it.' Now she did reach out to cover his hand with hers. 'Especially when I know your feelings about my dad.'

'That doesn't matter. My dad wasn't perfect either—he made some pretty bad choices in his life, but that doesn't alter his love for me or mine for him or how much I grieved for him. You loved your dad and he loved you—your grief is real and valid.' He took a deep breath. 'And whilst I do have issues with his choices, I do know they aren't your fault. From now on I'll act like that. Let's try and put the past behind us.'

'I'd like that.' A smile illuminated her face, though sadness still flecked her eyes. 'I really would.' Simultaneously they both seemed to realise that her hand still covered his and for a moment all he wanted was to increase that contact, to move round the table and hold her.

The desire caused a warning bell to klaxon in his brain. *Bad idea.* The knowledge hit him like an iced bucket of water on the head. Ava was grieving, was as vulnerable as he had been in the aftermath of his father's death. That meant her perspective would be skewed just as his had been. In his case he had ended up believing himself in love, had ended up in a marriage that had been a mistake. Guilt touched him. Maybe he should never have asked Ava to be part of this charade, perhaps in itself that had been taking advantage. But it was too late to change that now. All he could do was ensure he acted honourably and with sensitivity. That meant keeping their latent attraction in check and that in turn meant keeping their physical contact to a minimum. It would be all too easy for a hug to morph into something more. This he knew.

But perhaps he could try to make the sadness recede from her eyes—there could be no harm in that. 'Dessert?' he suggested. 'And then I suggest we should test each other on our fact cards.'

'Sure.'

'But let's make it a little more fun than a straightforward test.'

Now curiosity surfaced and sparked her eyes. 'How?'

'I'll get the dessert and I'll tell you.'

Ava watched as Liam stacked the plates in the dishwasher, her body and mind in turmoil.

Emotions swirled, grief and a warmth at having had that grief understood—a sense of a connection that somehow prompted her body to hum anew at the memory of earlier. Of being pressed back against him, his arm around her waist Just those few seconds seemed to have branded her in some way. And now...now she needed to get a grip, had to be careful.

They had agreed to put the past behind them but it still existed. Plus Liam was a widower—a man who hadn't dated since his wife died. And Ava wasn't on the market for a relationship with anyone. Yet when he returned bearing a dessert that looked utterly delicious she knew the adjective 'yum' was directed at him by her unruly hormones.

And somehow her gaze landed on a curl of his copper hair, shower damp on the nape of his neck, and it mesmerised her. She snatched her glance away only to land on the tantalising bare V of his neckline.

'It's one of Elena's specialities—' He broke off as he looked at her, must have read something in her gaze, or perhaps she was drooling or sending out some sort of smoke signal from her ears. But as he paused their gazes locked and she saw desire in the depths of his cobalt eyes.

Say something. Break the spell. 'Um...you

look amazing…' *Oh, for Pete's sake.* 'Not you. *It* looks amazing. The dessert, I mean.'

'So I don't look amazing?' Amusement laced his deep voice and she glared at him.

'I… I don't know.' Ava closed her eyes and wondered where twenty-seven years of poise had vanished to. Seemingly cancelled out by one curl of hair, some understanding, a sculpted face and an even more sculpted body and… There she went again.

'Sorry,' she said. 'I am a dessert sort of girl and this clearly fuddled my brain. It looks amazing. What is it?'

'*Barchiglia.* It's a chocolate and almond tart with a pear and sort of almond meringue filling.'

'That sounds to die for.'

'It is. That's why I thought we could use the dessert as a bit of an incentive.'

'How?'

'We cut it up into small pieces and every time we get a question right we get a piece. If we don't get it right we forfeit to the other person. And you really don't want to forfeit any of this.'

'Bring it on.' She watched as he cut the cake, appreciated the deft, confident movements, but even more she appreciated what he was doing—knew he was trying to distract her from her grief.

'OK. You ask first,' he said.

'What's my favourite colour?'

'Amber.'

'Correct.' He picked up a small piece and popped it into his mouth, and she smiled as he made an exaggerated *mmm* sound.

'My go. Where did I live as a child?'

'Surrey.'

'Also correct.' He pushed the plate towards her and she picked up a square of the confection. Nibbled it and closed her eyes. 'That is absolutely divine.' She took another small bite, savoured the taste of the almonds mixed with the tarter tang of the pears. Opened her eyes to find his eyes centred on her lips and she felt heat touch her face. Ate the last bit and returned to the questioning.

As the hour went on and the *barchiglia* reduced in size it became a challenge, both of them trying to find harder, more difficult questions until finally there was just one square left.

'All to play for,' he said.

'And it's my question.' She leant back in the chair, her eyes narrowed as she thought of a question that might flummox him. 'Name three products that I modelled.'

Liam paused, thought for a moment. 'Sahara clothes, Madeline cosmetics and…you were also the cover girl for lingerie, but the name of the company escapes me. Something to do with Temptation, I believe.' His voice was deep and husky as he said the word and she found herself leaning forward.

'It was called Allure.' And she couldn't help it, she said the word with a deliberate emphasis, and now the atmosphere seemed to cloud and haze with the simmering fog of tension. The urge to reach out, to touch, was almost too much. Almost.

He pushed his chair back, the scrape of wood against the marble dispelling the mist of desire. 'We need to talk about this.'

'About what?' The question was disingenuous but she needed to be sure she hadn't misinterpreted the signals.

'This chemistry. This attraction.' Against her will the words sent a small thrill of satisfaction through her. The idea that this desire was mutual, that he felt the same pull, the same yearning strummed a triumphant chord through her whole body. 'Because if we don't figure out how to deal with it, ironically it will undo our whole act.'

'You're right. So we need to work out a way to feel comfortable with the attraction.

Accept it and control it. Switch it on and off for the camera.'

'How?'

Ava inhaled a deep breath. 'First we need to get used to being in the same space. Let's give it a try.' His expression was so ludicrous she almost sighed, until she glimpsed her own reflection and saw the proverbial rabbit-in-the-headlights glint in her own eyes. 'We look terrified and that is *not* a good look for the camera. So let's start small. We need to smile.'

'Like this?' His lips turned up, the line forced and rigid but at least pointed in the right direction.

'That's not a bad start, but it looks a little forced and your eyes are still...' *shadowed, hard* '...not relaxed.'

'OK. Show me how it's done.'

'Easy. What sort of smile do you want? Girl next door, sultry, loving, flirty?'

'You pick.'

Ava closed her eyes for an instant and then smiled, a smile that she knew held a hint of fun, a touch of flirt and a dollop of come hither. 'So that's flirty. This is girl next door.' She widened her eyes and her smile, conjured up the idea of fresh-faced and wholesome. 'It's all about showing teeth without being toothy.'

'That's incredible.'

'I figured it out from a young age. I started family photo shoots when I was a toddler. I worked out the quickest way to get them done was to achieve whatever look the photographer and my mother wanted.'

And then she'd worked out the power of smiles—they could be used to impress people, to make people believe she was happy, to make other people feel good. A smile was a perfect disguise. She had learnt to keep her thoughts private and her smile on display. Hidden her hurt that she knew her mother's love was not really for her, for Ava. Her mother had loved her as long as she played her part. Her father would only love her as long as she was perfect. And so she'd smiled until her cheeks had ached and she'd looked perfect.

'But how does anyone know when it's genuine? How do *you* know?'

The question took her aback and as she considered her answer a level of discomfort tinged with uncertainty touched her. When was it genuine? Her smile, her façade so much part of her daily life she didn't even think about it. 'Because I mean it.' The answer was lame and she could see he was about to question it. 'But that's not the point. It's your smile we need to focus on. Try again.'

This time the attempt was woeful and she raised her eyebrows. 'Is that really the best you can do?'

'Right now, yes. Perhaps you could pass on some helpful tips.'

'Think of something happy.'

Liam looked up at the ceiling and then a smile did tip his lips, but it was not a smile that implied relaxation or joy. There was a grimness to it, an edge that held more than a hint of danger. A smile that sent a shiver down her spine.

'What are you thinking of? I mean, that's better but not exactly what I was after. That's more the smile of a man who has won a fight.'

Two raised eyebrows and a nod. 'Ten out of ten. I was picturing AJ's face when I win the Beaumont contract.'

'OK. But now try for a different sort of happy. Maybe think of a more relaxing activity than a fight. Such as...' Oh, hell, the only image that entered her head right now was definitely not appropriate. 'Um...think of chocolate.'

'Chocolate?' The word was flat.

'Yup. Doesn't chocolate make you happy?'

'Not really. I mean, I like the occasional chocolate orange, but I wouldn't say that would make me smile.'

'OK. What do you do to relax?'

'The gym. Or I may work out in the ring, or do some sort of obstacle marathon.' He sighed. 'I'm guessing that's not what you're after.'

'No. I was thinking more about bubble baths or watching a film on a rainy day or lying on a beach.' Now she sighed. 'Let me guess. You're more a shower sort of person.'

'Afraid so. I don't think I've had a bubble bath since I was a kid.'

'Then we'll have to try another method. There was a time on a shoot when I couldn't get the smile right. It was one of my last assignments.' Her dad had just got out of hospital after his first heart attack, her world had been turned upside down and she'd been angry, sad and scared. 'There was a coach who helped me.' She gestured. 'Stand up and smile.'

He did as she asked and she stood and moved closer to him, told herself this was necessary. Any minute now she was sure her brain would find the off switch and in the meantime she'd focus on keeping her breathing even.

'Hold still. It's all about your mouth and facial muscles and knowing which ones to relax. You're too tense. Try to relax.' Telling herself this was purely professional, utterly clinical, she reached up and touched his jaw. 'Clench and relax your jaw a couple of times.' The feel of bristle under her fingertips, the sheer strength and determination of him made her clasp her lip between her teeth. No way would she actually moan.

She dropped her hands to his shoulders, both left and right. 'Drop your shoulders.' Now their bodies were scant inches apart and she tried to breathe normally. Knew this was playing with fire.

She could hear how breathless her voice was and when she met his gaze she saw a spark ignite there, his cobalt eyes darkened and she knew he was as affected as her.

'Anything else?' he asked, his voice more croak than depth.

'You need to engage the muscles round your eyes. Try crinkling them slightly.'

'Ava.' The smile, real or fake, had dropped and there was a seriousness to his expression that made her breath catch. Her brain ordered her to move backward but somewhere down the line the command got confused and instead she stepped forward.

'Another tip is to massage your forehead and cheeks and…' She was now so close she could smell the bergamot of his soap, could see the slightest dent in the sweep of his nose, the hint of a seldom seen dimple, and her voice ran dry, shuddered to a stop as she took the final step forward.

Then she wasn't sure who kissed who, but his lips were on hers and it felt as if her body were melting, fusing with his as she pressed against him, wrapped her arms around his neck as he deepened the kiss. It was as though she'd been waiting for this ever since that first kiss, the feeling of rightness inexplicable.

Her senses competed and then soared into sensory overload, the experience blew her mind, as she tasted the hint of wine, of chocolate, of almond, felt her tummy clench in the need for more. More of this exquisite, gorgeous torture. Torture because she could hear the voice of common sense clamouring, knew that the need for more was doomed to failure, knew that what she had to do now was pull away.

As she suited action to word they stood, her breath coming in ragged gasps, and she could see the rise and fall of his powerful chest as they stared at each other and Ava knew no amount of poise could rescue her now. Mortification suddenly roiled through her. That had been a disaster, a complete loss of the composure she was famed for. Hadn't she been the one to advocate acceptance and control? But perhaps, just perhaps, she could rescue the situation, use every iota of her acting skills. Somehow she forced herself to raise her head and meet his gaze.

'Sorry about that.' She searched her bank of smiles and came up with rueful, embarrassed, but hopefully with at least a semblance of sophisticate. 'That is obviously not the "look" we are going for. Bit too full on. I was hoping we could practise the sort of kiss that looks good for the cameras. I didn't expect us to get so…carried away. It's a while since I've been in a relationship so it was obviously some sort of strange reaction to that.'

There was a moment's silence and she thought he'd challenge her assertion, force an admission that she'd kissed him because she couldn't help herself. Then, perhaps realising there would be nothing to gain, he nodded and his body relaxed. 'Well, it certainly brought a smile to my face.'

Recognising his attempt to relax the atmosphere, she smiled, this one of relief. 'On that note, I think we should call it a day now and regroup in the morning.'

'Agreed. I'll see you then.' Hard to say who ran for the door faster.

CHAPTER SEVEN

LIAM OPENED HIS eyes and as always went from sleep to awake in an instant, his brain scanned the surroundings for danger and landmarks—a trait honed in his army days, part training and part defence against AJ and his bully-boy cronies.

Today though a different type of danger pervaded the air, in the shape of a beautiful woman who had aroused a storm of passion in him. Perhaps Ava had it right—the kiss had been a simple scientific release of pent-up need; neither of them had kissed anyone else for a long time. Perhaps if he kept telling himself that he'd believe it.

A quick shower and he headed to the kitchen, where breakfast was laid out and the scent of coffee permeated the air. Ava turned and smiled. 'Elena left us all this. It looks amazing.' She waved him to a seat. 'Sit. I'll bring the coffee over. I thought you could tell me a bit more about Rourke Securities over breakfast.'

'Sure. What do you want to know?'

'How did you start?'

'After I left the army...' he'd crawled into an abyss of self-pity, grief and self-recrimination, had finally pulled himself out '... I set myself up as a one-man security band.' Lured by danger, fuelled by adrenalin, he'd accepted assignments where death had been a constant risk, the only way he could feel alive. Until injury had halted him in his tracks and his old army commander had made him rethink his path. 'It grew from there. I built a team of operatives and it spiralled. I branched out into non-military contracts. I bought a fleet of vans and started a transportation sideline that grew and grew. Then I started offering security for events and so it went on. And here I am.'

'Starting your own business, making it yours...that must be...fulfilling.' She sounded wistful. 'That feeling of achievement, of building something on your own.'

'Sounds like that is what you would like to do.'

Her look was slightly defiant. 'I've thought about it. I mean, I know how lucky I am—but sometimes it does feel like I've been handed everything on a silver platter. I wonder if I could have achieved success on my own.'

Liam considered. 'I'm not sure it matters. There are different parameters of success. You could take Dolci on to bigger and better things, make a success of it your way, with or without the Petrovellis. You could count your modelling career as a runaway success—that was down to you.'

'Not really. That is down to genetic luck and, let's face it, my connections probably helped me.'

'You are who you are and life deals you the cards it deals you—all you can do is play the best hand you can. Is heading up Dolci what you want to do?'

'Yes.'

'Then do it to the best of your ability. If you had started Dolci, what would you do with it?'

'I'd like to grow the company differently, sell more organic, fair trade produce. Be way more ethical. I'd also like to set up some small high-street shops that sell our products. Maybe even launch out from desserts to a few good quality ready dinners for families and people who live on their own.' She grinned. 'Kind of like Elena's food, but in bulk. I know it will lose some of its authenticity if it's mass produced but I'd do everything I could to keep it as "real" as possible.'

The ideas poured out of her, the spark in her eyes, the way she moved her hands to emphasise a point exuded a vibe or energy, piqued his admiration and interest.

'Then that's what you should aim for. Look into those ideas.'

'Maybe.' But the enthusiasm had gone and now she rose to her feet. 'Anyway, enough of that—it's more information than you need and definitely more than I meant to say. You should have stopped me.'

'I didn't want to stop you. I enjoyed listening. You are full of ideas—good ideas.'

'Thank you.' But he could see she hadn't taken the words on board, wondered why someone like Ava Casseveti found it so hard to believe in herself. 'So what's the plan for the day?'

'My idea for the day was to go into town. Practise being seen and spending time together so it starts to look natural.'

'Then give me ten minutes to get ready and let's go.'

CHAPTER EIGHT

AVA CHECKED HER reflection in the pretty full-length mirror in her bedroom and gave a satisfied nod. The white dress with the poppy-red pattern was perfect: swirly, flirty, fun and it made her look good without being overtly revealing or too noticeable. Topping it with a fleece-lined denim jacket for warmth, she would blend into the tourist crowd. She tugged her trademark blonde hair into a ponytail. One last swipe of lip gloss, a press of her lips, and she exited the room and headed downstairs. Twenty minutes later they were on the cobbled streets of the town and Ava gasped as she took in the architecture of the buildings.

'I had read about the *trulli* but the pictures don't do them justice.' She halted to appreciate the sheer unique quality of the small stone whitewashed buildings topped with conical roofs. 'They are straight out of a fairy tale.'

'Maybe they are—they were built centuries ago, just in this part of the world as far as I know. Some people believe they were built in order to avoid tax.'

Ava turned to him in question. 'I assumed they were houses or storage units.'

'The story goes that the King charged the local lord a dwelling tax. So they figured out a way of building dwellings that could be dismantled whenever the tax inspector paid a visit and put back up when he left.'

'Ingenious.' She gazed at the cluster of buildings. 'I can't believe they are still standing.'

'Yup. It does show that, for all the gains we have made with technology, there are still plenty of structural wonders that come from our history. And these definitely count.'

'Do people still live in them?'

'In some of them, but they are mostly used for commercial purposes—shops, restaurants or holiday lets.'

'Could we go to the shops? I'd like to pick up some gifts before we meet your family tomorrow.' The idea rippled nerves through her and she reminded herself that it was essential to do a 'meet the family' with Bea before their relationship became properly public.

As they made their way along the sun-drenched streets she sensed his glance and turned to look at him. He nodded towards a couple walking ahead of them, arms draped around each other's waists. 'In case we are spotted, and also as a kind of practice, do you think we should…hold hands?'

Ava bit her lip. 'Yes. You're right. We should.'

'Yet you didn't suggest it. And you're the detail guy.' His cobalt gaze held a perception that was becoming all too familiar. 'So I'm guessing the idea doesn't appeal, which is fine by me.'

Ava hauled in breath. 'No. You're right. It's a good idea. It shows affection and proves we are close. I'm just a bit funny about it. I remember being asked to hold hands for a modelling shoot—the idea was to show a married couple's intimacy and it made me re-alise there *is* something really intimate about it.' It had also made her question her own ca-pacity to be intimate. Because after that shoot she had realised that she and Nick never held hands. Because it hadn't ever felt natural. 'I guess there's also a bit of worry. I mean, what if your hand is sweaty, or uncomfortable to hold or…?' She held her hand out and sur-veyed it. 'And now I've managed to make something insignificant into something huge.'

'Nope. I think you're right.' He frowned and she sensed a sudden pain in his voice, wondered if he was remembering walking hand in hand with Jess. 'Holding hands is intimate. It links you, creates a connection, an implication of a bond, a desire to be close. It's also a way of communicating—you can squeeze someone's hand to show support or commiseration or in warning. So yes, it is a big thing and maybe that's why some people don't feel comfortable with it. If we were really a couple I guess we'd both have taken a while before we felt ready to hold hands.'

'But we have now supposedly been together for three months and it would be a bit strange if we didn't hold hands.' Yet she'd been with Nick for eighteen months and hadn't held hands even once. 'So we're going to have to do it.'

'Maybe, but not now.' Liam indicated ahead of them. 'This shop looks like what you're looking for.'

It did indeed. The whitewashed *trullo* was bedecked with vivid hand-painted signs and wooden shelves stacked with intriguing pottery that tempted the eye. They entered the shop and Ava gave a small cry of delight. The shop was filled with local items, textiles of every hue, ceramics painted with vivid imagery, miniature *trulli* completed in exquisite detail, alongside black and white photographs of the village in times gone by. 'It's like a treasure trove.'

The proprietor stepped forward. 'Many of the items have been made by local artisans. The linens have been hand-woven and there are also some beautiful examples of filet lace.'

'They are all beautiful.' She turned to Liam. 'Let's start with your mum.'

'Um…' He glanced round, a slightly helpless look on his face. 'We don't usually do holiday gifts.'

'Yes, well. This is different. You're bringing a girlfriend home. And not any old girlfriend. A Casseveti. Your mum will hardly be thrilled to see me—the least we can do is take her and the rest of the family gifts.' She picked up a jug, beautifully hand crafted with a picture of a rooster and a flower on the side.

'Maybe not that. The symbols represent fertility.'

Ava placed it down hurriedly. 'OK. But there is plenty to choose from. What did you get her for Christmas?'

'Mum sorts out the gifts for me—she tells me what everyone would like and I give her the money.' He shifted from foot to foot.

'That way everyone gets what they want. Seems easier.'

'OK. But you must have some idea. What does she like? What makes her smile? What's her favourite colour? Does she have any hobbies? Does she like clothes?' Ava walked over to a selection of beautiful patterned scarves. 'Perhaps a scarf?'

Now finally she saw Liam engage as he studied the scarves. 'She is very elegant,' he said finally. 'She always made a point of looking good. She'd go out and scour the charity shops and find amazing things. She even taught herself how to make her own clothes.'

He tugged his phone out of his pocket and Ava looked at the photograph. Liam's mum was pretty, her copper hair faded with age, but her grey eyes were still bright. Her smile was slightly wary, but there was a serenity about her that Ava liked. She studied her clothes. Elegant grey skirt with a white blouse. Nice and simple, but livened up by a bright red cardigan.

'I think she'd definitely like a scarf or some jewellery. You pick.'

Liam studied the items on display, picked a couple of scarves up and held them to the light, chose a dark red patterned one. 'I think she'd like this.'

'Perfect. Now for my mum.' Ava sighed. 'I wish I could get her a magic wand that would make her feel better. Less miserable.' Less vindictive, less angry... Perhaps she could cast a spell that would somehow make her mother forgive Ava for refusing to try to overturn the will.

Liam pointed at a display of crystals. 'Maybe a crystal—some people believe that crystals have healing properties or can help in times of grief.'

'Do you believe that?' The man really was a whole heap of surprises.

'I don't know. I do think that it is possible.'

'I think that's a brilliant gift.' Ava looked at the crystals and then back at him. 'I don't think Mum is a believer but I think I'll get one anyway. Maybe they work even without belief.' She tried to keep sadness from her voice, knew she'd failed when he looked more closely at her.

'I assume she has taken it hard. Every article I ever read showed how close your parents were.'

'Yes.' No way would she expose the illusion her mum had so painstakingly set up, tell Liam that her father had still loved his first wife, just not enough to stay with her. Had loved Karen's money and connections more, but hadn't loved Karen herself. Sometimes Ava wondered if it had been worth it—he had sacrificed love to live a life cushioned by money, but also trapped by it. The fate of Dolci caught up in his marriage, in the Casseveti brand. And so he'd been a prisoner of his own ambitions. Had he ever just wanted to break free, abandon his second family and return to his first?

'I'll get Mum this as well.' She picked up a simple terracotta jug. 'I think we should get something for your stepdad and brother as well.'

'I really wouldn't have a clue what to get John or Max. I never lived with them and there is no blood tie so we aren't close.' There was an emptiness to his tone, a careful flatness, and his eyes held trouble in their depths.

'I know you didn't choose their gifts but you must have watched them open them.' His expression was one of reluctance and a sudden suspicion touched her. 'I mean, you did spend Christmas there, didn't you?'

'I popped in a few days after.' He rubbed the back of his neck. 'I was away over Christmas.'

'Where did you go?'

'Business trip.'

'On Christmas Day?'

'Yes. I was in a five-star hotel in India and that was fine.' His stance suggested the subject was closed. 'But looking back, I do remember that Max thanked me for my gift. I got him a pair of Rollerblades. He is roller skating mad. He plays roller hockey and does speed skating. Works as a skate guard at a local rink.'

Ava pointed at a small table with trays of beaded bracelets. 'Look. They look cool and I bet he could wear that to rollerblade.'

They walked over to them and she watched as Liam went through the merchandise, a small frown of concentration on his face. 'I'm pretty sure the Rollerblades were this colour, so this should work.'

'What about John?'

'I'll buy him some Italian beer or some interesting food ingredients. He does a lot of their cooking.'

'Good idea.' It occurred to Ava that in actual fact Liam knew more about John and Max than he cared to admit, or perhaps even realised. She waited whilst Liam paid for his purchase.

'Where would you like to go now?' he asked.

'I thought we should get some photos of us. We can post them on social media as evidence of our relationship. I think that's the best way to let people know—a kind of subtle approach, rather than an official announcement.'

'Makes sense.'

'Where would be a good place for some photos? I was thinking somewhere romantic.' A flush heated her cheekbones. 'Just for the detail.'

'How about a beach setting? There is a beach not too far from here though I've never been. It's a nature preserve, so it's fairly secluded.'

'Sounds perfect.'

'I'll call Pierre to drop us off.'

CHAPTER NINE

An hour later they stood and stared at the expanse of beach. White sand stretched before them, sloping to the near transparent turquoise of the sea, dappled and flecked by droplets of the February sunlight.

'This is absolutely beautiful,' Ava breathed.

'Yes.' But Liam realised he wasn't looking at the view. Instead his gaze had settled on Ava and something tugged inside him. *She* looked beautiful, her blonde hair ruffled by the breeze, her wide amber eyes entranced by the scenery. *Get a grip. Think of some facts.* 'It's a protected area so there are no beach bars or any developments allowed.'

'It's an ideal setting for some photos. I am going to do a collage and then post them up with a suitably cheesy message. Let's start simple, pose sitting on those rocks over there.'

They made their way across the sand and the feel of it crunching between his toes, the fresh sea breeze, all instilled a sense of calm. Dispelled the thoughts of his mum and John and Max, the reminder of Christmases spent away to allow them the space to have a proper family Christmas. Unlike those they'd endured when Liam was a child, marred by the alcoholic rants of his father. The most memorable the time Terry Rourke had flung the turkey at the wall. They reached the rocks and she sat down and inhaled a deep breath. 'How about we sit quite close, look at each other and make funny faces?'

'Funny faces.' Despite his best effort Liam could feel his face pull itself into a scowl, the thought of looking like an idiot not one he relished.

'Yes. You know. Kind of playful and like we're having fun.'

'No. I don't know. I've never taken a selfie and I haven't pulled a funny face since I was a kid.'

Ava stared at him. 'Never taken a selfie. Ever?'

'Nope. I run a security firm—social media isn't my thing. I'm more of a low-profile kind of guy.'

'It's not just about social media—I take loads of selfies with friends because it's nice to have quickly accessible memories. Look.

I'll show you the sort of thing I mean.' She rose lithely to her feet and he caught his breath. She stood straight and slender, the dress she wore floated in the breeze in a swirl of colour, one hand caught her hair back to keep it from her eyes and in that second he got what she meant. Wanted a picture to capture this memory.

Desire tugged at his gut, but it was more than a physical need. Her smile, the teasing glint in her eyes combined, made him want to catch her in his arms, twirl her round, see laughter illuminate her face. *No point.* Once the charade was over he and Ava would go their separate ways and he would gain nothing from staring at a picture that simply marked an illusion. This wasn't real. Yet for one poignant instant he wanted it to be. The very idea caused a trickle of panic, urged him to flee, to distance himself from temptation.

Focus. Liam Rourke didn't flee, he fought, and he would do that now. Would remain calm and still, wouldn't let Ava so much as suspect the sheer stupidity of his emotions. Yet he couldn't keep his brows from lowering into a frown at his own idiocy. How could he even contemplate a relationship with Ava? A vulnerable woman caught up in grief and complexity. The last thing she needed was man who had no idea how to navigate the shoals of a relationship. Come to that it was the last thing he needed. His relationship with Jess had been a mistake from start to finish. His mistakes had compounded, one after another and ended in tragedy. Never again would he take that risk.

'Here we go.' Ava tilted her phone and he pulled himself to the present. 'These are the sort of selfies I take—because they're fun.' She scrolled down and he saw images of Ava with a pretty dark-haired woman. They were both beaming at the camera and the other woman was making a gesture over Ava's head. In another they were posing, dressed in pyjamas, a big bowl of popcorn next to them.

'That's Emily,' she explained. 'She's my best mate. This is the sort of thing I'm looking for—a fun photo. So you need to stop channelling your grumpy-old-man mindset and give this a try.'

'Grumpy old man?' Belatedly aware that his face was now set in a scowl, though not for the reasons Ava believed, Liam tried to change his expression to relaxed.

'Yes,' Ava said firmly. 'Though actually perhaps that is an insult to grumpy old men. Come on, Liam. Selfies are part of our world and it's time we got some evidence that you know how to have fun.'

'I do know how to have fun.' Was that a hint of gritted teeth he could hear in his voice?

'Prove it.' The challenge in her voice was unmistakeable. 'When was the last time you had fun? And work-related events don't count.'

Dammit. Liam racked his brains, and didn't like the answer that kept coming up no matter how much he ransacked his memory banks. Last time he could remember having fun was with Ava, laughing, talking and then, of course, those two kisses. But before that... He was coming up blank. 'This is a daft conversation.'

'In other words you can't come up with anything. Can you?'

'I am having a temporary memory blank.' For Pete's sake—his brain didn't even seem capable of making up anything fun.

Ava glanced sideways at him; a mischievous smile played on her lips. 'Then let's start now. I'll race you to the waves. Last one there pays a forfeit.'

Before he could even factor in the challenge she was off and running and he wasted further seconds caught flat-footed watching her as she sprinted forward, hair streaming behind her.

Quickly he started after, marvelled at her speed on the sand that seemed to slow him down, and Ava got to the cerulean sea with a couple of seconds to spare, turned to watch him, laughter in her eyes and on her lips as he reached her. 'I win,' she crowed and he gave a sudden laugh.

'So what's my forfeit?'

For an instant her gaze snagged on his lips and he knew what she wanted to suggest, could see it in her eyes, in the unintended provocative tilt of her body towards him, the instinctive step forward and then she shook her head, a small decisive admonition to herself.

'A funny face. You need to pull a funny face.'

That made him pause as he thought about it. 'What sort of funny face?'

'Any sort. Like this.' She stuck out her tongue and put her hands to the side of her face and wiggled her fingers.

'Fine.' Feeling like a complete idiot, he copied her actions, was rewarded by her spontaneous peal of laughter. He stepped forward into the water, felt the cold swish of the waves as they covered his toes. Without thinking he held out his hand and she took it, and together they stepped forward until the water reached their knees.

He turned to her, looked down at their clasped hands and their previous conversation unrolled before him. Following his gaze, she too stared down and for a moment it all felt too intimate, too close, and then before it could morph into awkwardness Ava smiled.

'It's OK. Let's not overthink it. Let's use this as the perfect photo opportunity.' Gently she dropped his hand and moved closer to him. 'You need to put your arm round my waist.' But now all he could think about was her closeness, how right it felt, and the panic resurged; his brain felt fuzzed by the conflict of emotion inside him. A desire to hold her close, a yearning to kiss her buffeted the knowledge that this was all wrong. A mirage.

Carefully, gingerly, he did as she said; his heart hammered his ribcage, and nerves and anticipation tightened a band across his chest as her arm slipped round his waist. His pulse pounded as her corn-blonde hair tickled his nose and a series of images flashed through his brain. All of Ava, in the shop, laughing as she raced over the sand, her expression when they'd kissed, her response, the sensations. Everything fused into an intensity of reactions and as she looked up at him, he smiled, just as the camera clicked.

He didn't want to move, wanted to gaze on her upturned face, lean down and taste those lips, lips that enticed and tempted. The instant froze in time; it seemed to stretch and pull to urge him to act. He blinked, tried to break the spell and now she dropped her arm from his waist. Stepped back slightly shakily and shook her head so her hair hid her expression. Turned slightly away to study the photograph.

'Look. It's pretty good.'

Ava was right. It was good; any observer would see what they were supposed to see. A relaxed couple smiling each other. A qualm struck Liam—his smile was genuine, whilst Ava's had obviously been her model's pose, an illusory rictus. The knowledge felt stupidly bleak and he forced a lightness to his voice.

'Not bad. I've got the hang of this. Maybe I should sign up with an agency.'

'They'd snap you up,' she agreed, matching his tone, though her expression was still partly obscured. 'A few more and I think we're good to go.'

'Excellent. I'm not sure about you but I am hungry. There's an amazing pasta place in town if you fancy it?'

'Sounds good.'

* * *

And so a few photos later Pierre picked them up and took them back to the town and Liam led the way to small, discreet restaurant. 'You get great food in the more touristy places but, according to Elena, this is the best place to eat in all the town.'

'It smells incredible,' Ava said as they followed a waiter to a small table in the window. She looked around, took in the simple rustic interior, the wooden tabled topped with jugs filled with sheaves of wheat.

'The pasta is all handmade in our kitchens,' the young man explained as he handed them menus. 'From Cappelli wheat, which is both delicious and healthy. It used to be known as "meat for the poor".' Another smile and, 'I'll be back in a few minutes for your orders.'

'Thank you.' Ava studied the menu and frowned. 'I may as well just close my eyes and jab. They all sound incredible.' Quickly she suited action to word. 'I'm going to have the *laganari alla Martinese*. Dry-cured ham, dates, local cheese and exotic-sounding mushrooms.' She glanced at him, saw that his gaze held both amusement and warmth and for some reason she felt colour rise to her cheeks. 'What about you?'

'Why don't you choose for me? You could use the same method.'

She looked at him suspiciously. 'Why?'

Now he smiled and the heat deepened. 'Honestly? I want to watch you do it again. You had a really serious frown and you look like you probably did when you were a child opening her Christmas presents.' He gestured to the menu. 'And it seems as good a way as any to choose.'

She shook her head. 'Then you do it. And I get to watch you.'

He raised his eyebrows in an exaggerated movement and she replayed the words. 'OK. That sounds a little weird, but go ahead.'

His broad shoulders lifted in a shrug and then he closed his eyes and for that instant Ava took the opportunity to study his features. The strength and determination of his jaw and the thickness of his dark eyelashes. His finger hovered and then descended and he opened his eyes. '*Sagna al baccala*. Salt cod and pine nuts and broad beans. I like it.' Now suspicion tinged his tone. 'You didn't take a photo for your collage, did you?'

'No, but I should have.'

'I'm not doing it again,' he said firmly. 'You have enough photos.' Once the waiter took their orders he looked at her. 'What exactly will you do with them?'

'We need to talk about that,' she said, and for a moment she felt a sudden pang of regret. Instead she wanted to discuss the menu, the weather, what books she liked, films, music. *Like a date? A real date?* Was that what she wanted? A small swirl of confusion spiralled in her—the very fact she had to ask the question generated further panic. She had to get a grip. This was fake and she had to remember that. The very last thing she wanted was a relationship with a man who was still in love with his dead wife. All that could lead to was misery. Her own mother had fallen for a man in love with his first wife and had spent her whole life striving to keep him, lived in fear of losing him. But with Liam Ava would already have lost.

'Go ahead,' he said and she pulled herself to the present.

'Well, once we do the "meet the family" tomorrow I'll start posting the photos on social media.' She hesitated. 'I'm not quite sure what may happen next but I think you need to be prepared.'

'Prepared for what?'

'There may be quite a bit of publicity. I've been in the press recently and in the past.'

'Exactly. That's kind of the point.'

'Yes.'

Liam looked at her. 'What am I missing?'

'It's not a lot of fun. I've spent most of my life in the public eye and it's…intrusive.'

'OK. Define intrusive.'

Ava hesitated. 'Let's say we get asked to do an interview for a glossy magazine. They will ask questions.'

'Sure. Like our first date and where we met, et cetera, et cetera.'

'Yes. But they won't stop there. They will also ask about our past and that will include past relationships.'

'Oh.' Liam exhaled a sigh. 'Of course it will. I should have realised that.'

Ava could see his discomfort at the very idea and she didn't blame him. In the past days he had barely mentioned his wife at all and she sensed for Liam his marriage was intensely personal.

She sat back as the waiter approached and served their pasta dishes, smiled her thanks and waited until he was out of earshot.

'It's not just the questions—there will also be interest. People taking pictures, people talking about us, and it won't always be positive commentary. When you're part of a couple people seem to think they have the right to comment on your private life, assess your every move.'

'You're speaking from personal experience.' Liam frowned. 'Your last relationship was pretty high profile, wasn't it?'

'Yes.' Ava took another forkful of her pasta, focused for a moment on the sheer pleasure experienced by her taste buds in the hope it could counter the bitter taste generated by thoughts of her last relationship. Another mouthful and she sighed. 'On that note I suppose we should share some information about our past relationships. A real couple would have done that by now.'

He nodded, his face unreadable apart from a grim twist of his lips.

'I know it will be very hard for you to discuss Jess, and I'm truly sorry. Please know I am not trying to pry.'

Another nod. 'I get that.'

'I may as well go first.' She sensed from his silence that he needed time to gather his thoughts. 'How much do you know? It was a fairly well publicised romance.'

'If I remember right he was a producer or something to do with acting.'

'Yes. His name was, well, still is, Nick Abingworth and he was every girl's dream. Handsome, charming...he had the ability to make you believe you were the world to him. He was an on-the-up producer—he'd done a very successful series and was about to film the next season. Just beginning to get some recognition. I was the perfect girlfriend for him.' Her gaze met his and now she allowed her lips to turn up in a cynical smile. 'For all the same reasons I am the perfect one for you. I was famous, I raised his profile, I had the connections he wanted, and I came from money.' The reminder of exactly why they were sitting there was a welcome one. 'He was trying to get a new project off the ground so I did my best to help him—I partied, I introduced him to people, I was photographed with him, and I did everything I could to promote him.'

'It sounds like you did a lot for him. What did he do for you?'

A small frown creased her brow. 'It doesn't work like that. I loved him, I wanted to make him happy, wanted us to work out, so I did my best to make that happen, be who he wanted me to be.'

His flinch was unmistakeable, as if her words had caused him physical pain, and then he shifted, reached for his fork, and she wondered if she'd imagined it. Then he said, his voice tight, 'But surely you should just have been yourself.'

'That was me being myself.'

'But did you enjoy the parties, promoting Nick?'

'I… I didn't really think about that. It was the right thing to do so I did it. I mean, I like the occasional party but I'm more a "curl up in front of a film with a big bowl of popcorn" kind of girl really.' Not that she and Nick had ever done that. Somehow Ava had convinced herself that all the socialising, all the networking had only been temporary, that once Nick had achieved his goal they would settle into a 'normal' life, maybe even get married, have kids. Because she'd believed he loved her.

'What happened?'

'We broke up. I asked my father to invest in Nick's project and he refused. Said he didn't think it was viable.' Ava had been stunned and then furious. Especially when James Casseveti had explained his other reasons.

'I'm sorry, Ava, but I don't believe the project is viable. I also don't believe in Nick. I think he is using you.'

Her father's face had been unusually grim.

'I won't let that happen. You deserve real

love, a man who loves you—not your money, or your public persona, or your connections.'

It was in that moment that Ava had known with certainty that her father had married her mother for all those reasons, a confirmation of a suspicion she'd harboured and resisted all her life, and anger had heated her veins.

'Just because that's what you did it doesn't mean Nick is the same. It doesn't.'

She'd waited, hoped her dad would deny the accusation, would agree with her, but he hadn't.

'I'm sorry, Ava. I hope I'm wrong, but I won't back Nick's project.'

'Nick was devastated so I backed it myself.'

Used up a vast amount of her savings, gave him a lump sum and loaned him the rest. Told herself that there was a difference between buying love and trusting love. Told herself that Nick's easy acceptance of the money was all right, that she didn't want gratitude because, as he pointed out, he was giving her an opportunity to invest. Told herself that she was imagining a change in their relationship, a withdrawal from Nick.

'Then Dad had his heart attack. I gave up modelling to enter Dolci. Life changed and Nick couldn't handle it. Couldn't cope with my "emotional neediness" so he left.'

The flush of remembered humiliation touched her anew and she pulled herself back to the present, saw the understanding in his eyes as he watched her. Nick had only been interested in what Ava Casseveti could get him and she'd been taken for a fool. That wouldn't happen again.

'I'm sorry,' he said. 'But he sounds like a scumbag. You're better off without him.'

'Yes, I know.' But it hadn't felt like that at the time. Yet, 'But compared to what happened to you a break-up is nothing. My situation was sad, yours is tragic.' Without thinking, she reached out and placed her hand over his. 'I'm sorry to ask, but do you think you could tell me a little bit about your marriage? I know it must be painful but it will look odd if I don't know anything.'

There was a silence as he took the last sip of his sparkling water and then he nodded, as the sun vanished behind a cloud and a small shiver touched her. 'I get that. But how about we move on from here first? There's a bar a few streets away with a heated rooftop terrace—we can watch the sunset.'

The words held a sense of poignancy and she nodded.

CHAPTER TEN

As they walked across the now dusky streets Liam appreciated Ava's silence, appreciated too her closeness as they made their way through the residential area, along pavements decked with potted plants and shrubs. The idea of discussing Jess was both unwelcome and strange, because for years he hadn't spoken about her to anyone, his ill-fated marriage and its attendant grief and regrets for his own consideration only.

Now that had to change—Ava needed some information—the key would be to try and keep it factual. They entered the small *trullo* that housed another souvenir shop and followed the signs to the back where a makeshift bar was in place.

'What would you like?' he asked.

'A glass of white wine, please.'

He ordered the same for himself and then gestured for Ava to climb the narrow spi-

ral staircase before him. Once on the rooftop
he watched Ava as she took in the setting,
knew he had brought her here because she'd
love it, that speaking of her relationship must
have been painful. Anger swiped him at the
thought of the man who had used her, used
her money and position under the guise of
love, left her when she would have needed
him most. Even as guilt jibed, pointed out
that he too was using her, even if he was at
least being honest about it.

'This is stunning.'

The terrace was decorated with twinkling
fairy lights that illuminated the early evening
dusk. Potted evergreens and trellises arched
and they could see the rooftops of the *trulli*
spread below them. They were the only customers as they sat down at the small wooden
table near the comforting warmth of an out-
door heater to counter the February chill.

For a moment they sat in contemplation
of the view, sipped their wine and somehow
Liam found a certain peace and tranquillity.
'OK,' he said finally. 'Let's talk. Maybe if I
just tell you the facts.'

'Whatever works best.'

Liam stared out over the panorama. 'I met
Jess when I was twenty-one. I'd been in the
army for three years. My dad fell ill and I got

leave to come and look after him.' He could still remember his shock when he had seen how much his dad had suddenly deteriorated. 'The alcohol abuse had caught up with him. The last weeks were pretty bad. His brain cells were fried, his memory was shot. He got so confused, was living in a myriad of memories. My mum wanted to help, but by then she'd been gone a few years, had already remarried. And my dad refused to even let her cross the threshold. So it was down to me. That's when I met Jess. Or, rather, reconnected with her. We'd gone to the same school. I bumped into her at the doctor's, we got talking and one thing led to another. Turned out her granddad had been an alcoholic so she understood what my dad was going through.'

'And what you were going through.' Ava's voice was quiet but full of understanding.

'Yes.' And he'd mistaken that connection for a deeper one. He'd been lonely and sad and confused and Jess had been like a lifeline. But even then he'd never thought about marriage—hadn't really thought at all. He'd just been happy to have someone there.

'You fell in love.'

'Yes.' What else could he say? For a time he'd believed it to be true. A mistake that he would carry with him all his life. But as he looked at Ava's beautiful face, illuminated by the last rays of the setting sun, just for one insane moment he wondered if he would ever utter words of love again. Shook his head. Surely this story of his past should cement the knowledge that he would never be so foolish again. Couldn't, wouldn't take that risk. 'We had a very quiet wedding because it was so close to the funeral and then Jess came and lived with me nearer my barracks.' And Liam had determined to stand by his vows, to do as he had expected his mother to do. 'Jess fell ill whilst I was on a campaign abroad. I came back as soon as I could but there wasn't much time left.'

For a moment he was back there in the hospital, with the distinctive smell of disinfectant, the beep of monitors echoing in his ears. Jess, gaunt and pale, her blue eyes so large in the pinch of her face. Her smile so sweet.

'I'm glad you're here.'

'Of course I'm here, Jess.'

She'd tried to rise and he'd carefully moved her, propped her up against the pillows.

'There are some things I want to say, before...before it's too late.'

'Anything.'

'I just want to say I'm sorry. When we met

I rushed you into everything. I took advantage of you.'

He'd smiled through his tears. *'And I enjoyed every minute.'*

Her hand, so skeletally thin, had squeezed his.

'But that wasn't enough. You were grieving and confused, but I was so happy that you wanted to marry me, happy to be wanted, that I decided that didn't matter. That we could make it work, that you would grow to love me, because I'd be the perfect wife. I shouldn't have done that. I'm sorry.'

'I'm the one who is sorry. All these years I haven't been there for you and...'

'It's OK, Liam. I love you. I've always loved you and you have been an honourable man—you stuck by me and that has honestly meant the world to me. So please, Liam, don't beat yourself up—you did good.'

She'd dropped back on the pillow, her face lined with weariness.

'I'm glad I said all that. Thank you for coming back.'

The conversation was one he would never share with anyone. Instead he simply said, 'I was with her at the end and I am glad of that.'

'I'm glad of that for both of you,' Ava said, her voice gentle. 'And I'm sorry, Liam, sorry her life was taken so soon and the whole life you could have had together is gone.' She looked away from him, at the sky touched by the orange rays of the setting sun. 'Would you like another drink?'

'Thank you.'

'I'll be back in a minute.'

As Ava walked down the winding stairs past the vintage sewing machines sadness touched her, for Jess's life snuffed out so tragically early, but also for Liam. The haunted look in his eyes as he'd spoken of his marriage and his wife's death had been all too apparent, and underlined the fact that Liam had not got over Jess and most likely never would. The knowledge added an extra layer to her sadness, made her wish she could help him, made her wish...wish what?

That he weren't a man weighed with grief, that somehow this were a real date, an attraction that could be pursued in the hope of the possibility of a future. That way lay madness. Ava would not even set a toe on that path of delusion, take a single step on the way to one-sided love ever again. That would be nothing short of utter foolishness. She might as well put a target on her heart saying: *Break me now.*

So from now on she had to focus on the fact that this was fake, that the attraction between them couldn't be acted upon or built upon or go anywhere. Full stop. So she would go back upstairs and concentrate on making this the best fake relationship she could, paying her father's debt to the best of her ability.

With a smile of thanks to the bartender she headed back to the terrace, handed Liam his glass and sat back opposite him.

'Thank you.' He smiled at her. 'For this and for being such a good listener.'

'No problem. As I said, I am truly sorry you had to talk about it and I'm sorry that there will be intrusive questions from the press.'

'It's their job, I guess. Any ideas what they may come up with?'

Ava sipped her wine, ran through the possible scenarios in her mind. 'I suppose one question may be, "What was it about Ava that made you re-enter the relationship arena after the tragic death of your wife?"' She gazed at the darkening sky now only tinged with the very last of the sun's rays. 'Obviously that will be somewhat awkward and I'll do my best to turn the conversation.'

'How?'

Ava thought for a moment. 'I'll say something like, "Hey, guys, much as I would love to hear my virtues extolled, Jess's death was tragic and I'd much prefer to take the opportunity to highlight what readers can do to help with research for the terrible disease that took her.'"

Liam stared at her in evident admiration. 'That's a brilliant answer.'

'Thank you very much. It comes from practice. I've been in the public eye for as long as I can remember.'

'Did you enjoy it?'

'I got used to it, because it's all I've ever known. And hopefully it will come in handy now. I will do my very best to deflect questions about Jess where I can.'

'I appreciate that.'

Ava sipped her wine, glanced at Liam and without her even meaning them to the words spilled from her lips. 'Do you think you ever will have a relationship? A real one, I mean?' Once said, the words seemed to hover in the air and she shook her head. 'Sorry. I shouldn't have asked that.'

'It's OK. It's a fair question in the situation and easy enough to answer. No. I won't. I've built my life on my own and I like it that way. I don't want to rock the boat with a relationship.'

How could she blame him? 'I totally get that.' The fervency in her voice was too much and Liam raised his eyebrows.

'So you're not looking for a relationship either?'

'Nope. For now I've given up dating completely. Like you, I am genuinely happy on my own. Why would I want to complicate that with a relationship?'

'Because you want the traditional happy ever after, kids, family life?'

All the things he must have once been looking forward to and had had taken from him.

'I don't know,' she said honestly. 'I do want that but only with the right person and I don't know how to figure out who that is.' She'd got it wrong once and she'd seen the unhappiness that could be generated by a bad marriage. 'Getting it wrong is not a risk I want to take.'

'But how will you ever work out who Mr Right is if you don't give anyone a chance?'

'That is an excellent question and yet another thing I haven't figured out.'

'Perhaps someone will sweep you off your feet.'

'Nope. No way. That sort of thing sounds all very well, but what if you get carried away by the moment and then you discover it's a mistake? When it's too late to get out.'

His expression changed and as he reached out for his glass his usually deft movement was a jerk that tipped his glass. Recovering, he caught it, lifted it and sipped. 'I think you need to take your time. Really get to know someone before you make a long-term commitment. But to do that you do have to go on that first date.'

'It feels too scary. Plus it doesn't work like that. However sensible you think you are you can get carried away—attraction, love…they can skew common sense, kid you into making stupid decisions.' As she had with Nick. 'I'd want to walk away the minute I felt my heart start beating a bit faster, the minute it felt even the tiniest bit out of my control.' She shrugged. 'It's easier to stay single.'

'Agreed. Though there are some drawbacks, unless you plan on a lifetime of celibacy.'

'That is a drawback.' The words seemed to whir across the table and take on a life of their own. Their gazes met and locked and her throat tightened. 'I assume you have no wish to join a monastery.'

'No.' He hesitated and then shrugged. 'The only solution I've come up with is an occasional one-night stand. One night means there is definitively nothing more than a brief physical connection.'

Ava looked at him. 'And that's enough?'

There was a silence and then he nodded. 'Yes,' he said finally as he drank the last of his wine. 'That is better than the risks involved in a relationship.' He shook his head, gave a sudden smile as if to lighten the mood. 'Listen to us. We are hardly advocates of true love. Yet we're about to try and sell the concept to the world. Or at least some of it.'

'It does sound a bit mad. But I just want to say. I…think we have a much better chance of pulling this off now. Italy was a good idea. It's given us a chance to get to know each other.' Which was a good thing, right? So why did it suddenly feel like a bad one?

She glanced at her watch. 'I guess we'd better get going. I need to pack and prepare. It's going to be a long day tomorrow.'

CHAPTER ELEVEN

THE FOLLOWING DAY, once again aboard the private plane, Liam surveyed Ava. As always she looked perfect, the outfit smart casual, dark blue jeans, tucked-in collared shirt topped by a pretty grey jumper with a floral edging, perfect for a meet the parent for the first time scenario. Her nails were a discreet neutral colour; her hair, freshly washed, cascaded in blonde waves past her shoulders and wafted an evocative floral scent across the table. Light make-up showed that she'd made an effort but without being over the top.

She frowned. 'Do I look OK? Should I have gone for something more businesslike?'

'You look fine. It's perfect for the occasion.'

'That's what I thought.'

He could see her nervousness though, the slight pallor of her skin and the amber flecks of wariness in her eyes. 'It'll be OK.' What else could he say?

'I hope so. I just know that this is going to be awkward.'

He hesitated, knew he was putting Ava in an unconscionable position. A few days ago it hadn't bothered him. Now scant hours away from bringing the two women together he felt...bad.

'You told me a bit about your mum. What about John and Max? What are they like?'

Edginess shifted inside him. 'Max likes rollerblading, he goes to school. He is a typical teenage boy, I guess. John works hard, he's quiet... I don't really know him that well. I was twenty when they got married. I...' The wedding was etched on his soul. When he'd seen the way John and Bea looked at each other, the love and joy in their eyes, their stance, their everything, seen Max wrap his arms round Bea's waist in a hug, Liam had realised with an intense visceral knowledge exactly what he'd cost his mother. That was when he'd vowed to stay clear, keep his distance, make up for what he had done. 'We're not really that close.' He tried for a smile, wanted to take the worry from Ava's eyes, rebury his own memories. 'It'll be OK. We go in, chat, leave. Look at it this way—if we can convince them, it will all be a breeze from there.'

'It feels like a pretty big if.'

'Hey, what's the worst that can happen?'

'I've considered that. How about this? Your mum sees through us in less than a minute… Your mum hates me because of my dad. Either way she throws me out.'

'Nah. Won't happen. My worst-case scenario is we succumb to the stress of it all and run around my mum's lounge clucking like chickens saying, "It's all a lie".'

The absurdity of the image caused her to give an involuntary chuckle. 'Speak for yourself. I guarantee I won't do that.'

A few hours later they pulled up outside a small well-maintained terraced house on the outskirts of London. Ava took in the bright red door, the clean paint on the walls, the small front garden replete with carefully tended flowers and shrubs. The elegant slatted blinds in the windows. 'It's lovely,' Ava said, though a part of her had expected Liam's mum to live in a larger house, had thought Liam would have given her a mansion.

As if reading her thoughts, Liam shrugged. 'It is. Though I did offer to buy Mum something bigger but she and John refused. Prefer to make their own way.' Impossible to be sure but she thought there was a hint of hurt in his tone.

Before she could reply he knocked on the door and sudden trepidation touched her. As if he sensed it, Liam took her hand in his just as the door swung open. A woman who was clearly Liam's mum stood at the door, a smile on her face. Her eyes went directly to Liam, rested on him for a poignant moment and Ava could see the love. Yet there was also a wariness, one that directly matched Liam's.

Liam moved forward, but she sensed an awkwardness in the jut of shoulder; for once his movement seemed stilted as he hugged the older woman.

'Mum, this is Ava. Ava, this is my mum.'

'Pleased to meet you.'

'And you.' Ava knew she had to avert the sense of discomfort in the air and it seemed clear that Bea felt the same way. The older woman smiled. 'John and Max are getting things ready in the kitchen. I thought maybe we should have a word in private first.'

Bea led them into the lounge, a tastefully decorated, comfortably cluttered room. She turned to Ava, her grey eyes clear and direct. 'Max knows nothing about what happened between your father and Liam's dad and I'd like to keep it that way.'

'I completely understand and I won't say anything about that,' Ava said, appreciating the directness of Bea's words. 'But I would like to tell you that my father did regret his actions. I realise that is not particularly helpful but he was sorry. And I am too.'

'Thank you. It was a long time ago now and, whilst I won't pretend to any positive feeling towards your father, I know his actions are not your fault. I will do my best not to make this awkward.'

'Thank you.'

She broke off as the door swung open to admit a youth and a tall man with grizzled hair and a serious face, though Ava noted his eyes held both warmth and humour. Both held trays containing tea and coffee pots as well as plates of cakes and biscuits.

'Ava, this is Max and John They have been baking up a storm today—sadly I am banned from the kitchen due to my non-existent baking skills. Which Liam will also attest to.'

Liam simply smiled, a small tight smile. 'I am sure these will be delicious.' But the words walked on stilts and Ava flashed a quick glance at him, instinctively stepped a little closer to him Irrationally wanted him to know that, whilst she definitely liked Bea, she was on his side. Though why there should be a side to pick, she wasn't quite sure.

Accepting a cake from Max, she smiled at him, saw he had inherited his dad's serious face. 'They are utterly delicious,' she said. 'Chocolate orange?'

Max nodded. 'Yes, and Dad made shortbread.'

'You are men of many talents.' She smiled at John. 'Liam did mention you love cooking and I understand Max, you rollerblade as well.'

The dark-haired boy nodded. 'I speed skate and I play roller hockey.'

Bea gave a small shudder. 'It's a pretty violent game. But Max is brilliant at it. He's trying out for the county team next week.' Her pride shone through and Ava could sense how close she and her stepson were, wondered whether Liam minded on some level. Impossible to tell from his expression, which was one of courteous interest.

Max turned to Liam and she could see the curiosity in his eyes. 'Um… We had a careers fair at school the other day. The army were there. It looked really cool. I… I told them about you.' Another quick look. 'They were talking about the army reserves. I wondered if you joined them. Mum said to ask you.'

Liam glanced quickly at his mum and then back to Max, and again Ava sensed an undercurrent of unease, suspected Liam wasn't quite sure what to say, what his mum wanted him to say. And her heart twisted inside her in empathy—she knew he wanted to do what was best. Knew too that Bea simply wanted him to tell the truth, otherwise she wouldn't have told Max to ask him. But perhaps what seemed obvious to her wasn't obvious to Liam.

Without thought she intervened. 'Liam told me he joined up because his boss at his Saturday job was in the reserves. That it was a great thing for him.'

Another glance at his mum and then Liam nodded. 'It gave me structure and I loved the physical side of it. I guess a gym would do the same thing but I liked the outdoors element. I made some good friends too—people I'm still in touch with today.'

'Maybe I'll give it a go. I'll mention you when I enrol.'

It became clear to Ava that Bea and John and Max were a happy relaxed family unit, the banter and the chat easy, and Ava found herself laughing at some of the dry anecdotes John told about work and some of the plumbing disasters he encountered. Yet throughout

Ava was, oh, so aware of Liam next to her, felt the palpable tension in his body, saw how little he participated. His laughter was a little forced, a beat behind everyone else.

And it tugged her heartstrings because this showed a vulnerable side to him and she wasn't sure what had caused that. Realising the topic had shifted once more, Ava quickly refocused.

'I've got to do some work experience as part of my course,' Max said. 'I wish I could roller skate for that. But I can't.'

'You could come to work with me.' Both John and Bea spoke at the same time and Max made a face.

'I really appreciate that but going to work with you or Dad isn't the same as...' He trailed off but Ava saw the quick glance that he cast at Liam.

So did Bea. Swiftly she leaned forward and Ava sensed it was to protect Max from potential rejection. 'We were wondering if you'd like to stay for dinner?'

'Another time,' Liam said. 'I've got plans for dinner tonight.'

For a moment a look of hurt flashed across Bea's face As if he too saw it, he said hurriedly, 'But definitely another time.'

'Definitely,' Ava added. 'And it's been so

lovely to meet you. I truly appreciate how welcoming you've been.'

Final goodbyes said, she followed Liam back to the car, climbed in and buckled up. 'We could have stayed for dinner if you wanted. I like them.'

'Yes. I could tell.'

Ava frowned, saw the closed expression on his face, sensed a taut undercurrent of emotion, saw the way his hands gripped the steering wheel.

'What's wrong?'

'Nothing.' He turned the key in the ignition and put the car into gear, each movement contained and yet she sensed that he wanted to crash and grind through the gears and accelerate away. Liam shook his head. 'There is just no point in them getting to know you too well—we're going to split up in a few months.'

For some inexplicable reason the words made her stomach dip, presumably at the idea of the media coverage of their split, the knowledge that they would have to manage it to minimise suspicion or negativity. 'Yes, but—'

'There aren't any buts. It's better to quit whilst we're ahead. We convinced them we're legit. Mission accomplished.'

For a moment Ava was tempted to let it

go—then she looked at him again, saw the shadow in his eyes and knew she couldn't do that. Perhaps it wasn't her business but she'd liked Bea. And John and Max. And it seemed all wrong that Liam didn't feel close to them. Didn't spend Christmas with them.

'Could we stop somewhere before you drop me back home? Maybe go for a walk?'

The glance he gave her held a wealth of suspicion and for a moment she wondered if he would refuse, simply press his foot on the accelerator, turn the music on loud and complete their journey. 'We need to discuss our plan for the next few days.'

'Sure. There's a large National Trust park nearby. We can head there.'

Twenty minutes later Liam surveyed Ava as they walked along a pretty tree-lined path; evergreens dense and green edged a garden that still bloomed with colour despite the winter month. She'd pulled on a navy-blue duffel coat and her cheeks were tinged pink from the breeze.

She glanced sideways at him and he recognised this as an unconscious indicator of a preliminary skirmish. 'The planning that must go into these gardens so they look beautiful all year boggles the mind.' Her tone was innocent.

'Yes,' Liam agreed. Where was she going with this?

'Do you garden at all?'

'Nope.'

'I think your mum and John do, though. I spotted their back garden and it's full of flowers and pots.'

'Yes.' He'd wondered if Ava had really brought him here to plan the next few days or to discuss their visit and now it seemed he'd been right to suspect the latter. 'But we aren't here to talk about gardening,' he said firmly. 'We need to think about our next steps.'

'Yes.' Now her chin jutted out determinedly. 'Which includes talking about family.'

'No need. We met my mum and her family and that box is ticked.'

'No, it isn't. What are you going to do if your mum follows up and asks us round for dinner?'

Liam sighed. 'Put her off? We can always be busy and I don't think she will ask again.'

'But that will hurt their feelings.'

'Perhaps. But that's better than her getting close to you and then we spilt up.'

Contrition touched her amber eyes and she reached out, placed a hand on his arm. 'I am *so* sorry. Your mum must have been devastated when Jess died—of course, you are trying to protect her.'

Liam blinked, saw the compassion etched on her face and knew he couldn't let her believe that.

'No. It's not that. Truly. Of course my mum was upset when Jess died. But they weren't close.' Jess had always said Bea made her nervous and in truth Liam had wondered if Bea had known, had seen that their marriage wasn't all it should be. After all, she had watched her own marriage disintegrate, perhaps she could see the signs. The idea had made him uncomfortable, had reinforced his decision to let Bea get on with her new life, protected from his problems. And Jess had seemed happy with that, happy for it to be 'just the two of them'.

'Then what is going on?'

'What do you mean?' He kept his voice even. 'Nothing is going on.' He tried to inject finality into his tone, but Ava shook her head.

'Yes, there is. Otherwise why were you so tense earlier?'

'I wasn't. Apart from being a bit nervous—this is the first time we've "appeared" in public as a couple.'

'I'm not buying that. You have nerves of steel.' She raised her hands up. 'If you want to tell me to mind my own business do, but don't lie to me.'

The words caused him to pause, swallow the words of denial that sprang to his lips. Dammit. He was lying. Irritation sparked inside him—this was exactly why he eschewed relationships. They became messy and complicated and he didn't know the correct responses. But lying didn't feel right and neither did the unvarnished truth. 'Fine. I wasn't nervous. We're just not close.'

'Why not?' The words impacted the air, directed by a force he didn't fully understand. 'I don't get it. Before I met them I thought maybe they weren't very nice but they are nice. All of them.'

'I know they are.'

'Then what's not to be close to?' Her face was serious, a wistful look in her amber eyes. 'You're lucky. Your mum, John, Max. They are lovely, decent human beings. I don't understand why you don't embrace the chance to be part of it. To ask Max to come and do work experience with you. Go have a beer with John. A cocktail with your mum. Celebrate Christmas with them all.' He heard frustration, almost anger in the vibrancy of her voice and he stopped in his tracks.

Ava stopped too, turned to him and he studied her face. 'Why does this matter so much to you?'

Now those amber eyes blazed at him. 'Because I'm angry that you're being so stupid. That you're wasting a chance to have a family. When I would do anything to have that opportunity. All my life I wanted siblings, real siblings, not a shadowy, furtive half-family I wasn't allowed to meet. I wanted a mum who I could be close to, laugh with, shop with, confide in. What I do have now are two half-siblings who won't even speak to me. And a mum who is furious with me. And you have this lovely family you are refusing to be part of.'

Understanding hit him; he heard the pain that underlaid her words, could see it in the way she turned away from him, tried to hide her expression. 'I'm sorry.' The words were wholly inadequate and they both knew it. 'I didn't realise.' Had always assumed the Cassevetis were a close, happy family.

'There is no reason why you should.'

'Do you want to talk about it?'

'It doesn't work like that. You don't get to hold back and not talk about your family stuff, whilst I discuss mine.'

'That's not how I meant it.' God. He really did suck at this. 'I just thought talking about it may help.' He stared at her as the penny dropped. Presumably that was exactly how

Ava felt too. She wanted to help him. The idea was startling in its novelty. And suddenly he did get it, knew that he wanted Ava to understand that he wasn't blithely refusing something she wanted so much. 'Shall we sit down and I'll try and explain?'

Ava shook her head. 'Hell. Now I feel like I've forced you into this.'

'You haven't. Truly.' She sat down next to him. 'You're right. My mum, John, Max... they are all lovely people and they are a happy family, a happy family unit. They don't need me to be part of it.'

'It's not about need. You could choose to be part of that happy family unit. You would be welcomed in.'

'It isn't that clear-cut. There's history.' He wanted Ava to know that she wasn't alone, that the past had thrown its shadow over his family as well. 'You know that my parents' marriage disintegrated.'

Ava nodded.

'Well, at the time I didn't know or fully understand what was going on, didn't realise how cruel a thing alcohol abuse is, how it changes a person. All I saw as a child was my mum trying to get my dad to stop drinking— she wanted him to "be a man", pull himself out of the pit of self-pity he was wallowing in. The problem was, the less sympathetic she was, the more he tried to convince her the blame was all your father's and the more bitter he got. And as Dolci really took off it got worse and worse. My mum kept telling him to let it go and he just couldn't.'

Ava's amber eyes focused on his face and he sensed how intensely she was listening to him. 'And the more you must have felt in the middle.'

'I wasn't as fair as that. I landed on my dad's side.'

'Because that way you didn't have to give up believing in him,' she said softly. And with such understanding he knew she truly empathised. Knew how hard she had worked at believing in her dad.

'Yes, but that meant I blamed my mother for not being supportive enough, not being loving or understanding enough.' He shook his head. 'What I couldn't see was everything she was doing. All the extra shifts, all the worries about not being able to pay the bills, and all the while having to deal with the demands of living with an alcoholic. But she always got on with it. There was food on the table, and she still made me do my homework. But my dad, he let me do whatever I wanted.'

'You were a child—a child doesn't understand the responsibilities of bills to pay or adult emotions. You just wanted everything to be OK, for your parents to be happy again.'

The sympathy in her eyes shivered discomfort down him. Little did Ava know how instrumental he'd been in his mother's unhappiness. He rubbed the back of his neck, knew he needed, wanted to tell her. 'Perhaps. But it didn't work out like that. Instead my mum met John when I was twelve. They fell in love.' Ava's eyes didn't move from his face, her whole being focused on him. 'She wanted to take me and leave Dad.'

'What happened?'

'Dad went nuts, and I took his side. I told her I wouldn't go, that I'd run away, quit school, that my dad would die without her and it would be her fault. I said so many things and in the end she stayed. For me.' His voice was bleak.

'You were a child. You loved your dad. What you did wasn't wrong. If your mother chose to stay with your dad that was her choice to make. It was not your responsibility.'

'I was still the reason she stayed. The reason she and John lost years of happiness and my mum gained years of misery. John met someone else, got married, had Max and Mum was devastated. It didn't work out because he'd never got over Mum. He and his wife got divorced and he got custody of Max.'

'But obviously they did reconnect.'

'Yes. When I joined the army Mum did finally leave Dad. A couple of years later she and John started talking again and very soon after that they got married.'

'That's a good thing.'

'Yes. It is. It's a wonderful thing and I am truly happy for them.'

Now her gaze held an awareness, an understanding that he didn't want. 'And you don't want to spoil it?'

'Yes… No. I don't want to intrude on it.'

'You wouldn't be. They like you. Your mum loves you. I could see all that.'

'In one visit?' He made no effort to hide his scepticism.

'Yes. I know what it feels like to have siblings who aren't accessible. Max looks up to you. I bet he'd love to have a hands-on older brother like you. You heard him when he was talking about the army. And joining the reserves. You're his stepbrother. Do something about it. Stop being scared. I know I'm right. They wouldn't feel you were intruding, they'd welcome you in. It's your family unit.'

For a moment her words slipped past all the barricades and guards, probed into a place he had blocked off long ago. He wondered what it would be like to be part of it, to fit in. Emotions dipped and waved. Envy? Sadness? Regret? Who knew? All he did know was that he didn't want to feel any of those emotions. Couldn't take the risk. Ava was right—he was scared. It was too easy to get it wrong. What if he encouraged Max to join the army and, God forbid, something happened to him? What if he somehow offended John and his mum had to take sides? Too many worst-case scenarios and he knew the best way forward was to make sure none of them were possible.

'Thank you for the advice, and I mean that. But I'm not a family kind of guy and I know they are happy, I know my mum is happy and that's what's most important to me. I'm not going to mess with the status quo. Because it's a good one.' He took a deep breath. 'But that doesn't mean you should do the same.'

'What do you mean?'

'Luca and Jodi—maybe you should try a different approach. Why don't you contact them direct rather than go through lawyers? Pick up the phone, leave messages, use social media. Talk to them.'

He wondered if his words even registered. Her head was shaking a denial before he'd even finished. 'I can't do that. The lawyers would have my guts for garters and my mum—I couldn't do that to her. She is already furious with me because I haven't tried to get the will overturned. She wants them out of our lives. I won't add to her sense of betrayal by doing something that would be a complete *et tu, Brute?* moment.' She rose to her feet, gave him a smile. 'Truly, it's better left.'

He knew the smile to be fake and the words to be wrong but what could he say? After all, wasn't her argument the exact one he'd advocated himself? *It's better left.* Conversations like this one tilted his ordered world, ones that reminded him exactly why relationships were a bad idea.

'Come on. I'll get you home.'

'Thank you. I'll post some photos on social media tonight. And I think from now on we need to be seen out and about a lot more. Dinners, parties, social events. I'll get it all set up.'

The business-like tone was exactly what he needed to hear.

CHAPTER TWELVE

LIAM OPENED HIS eyes the following morning, aware that he'd slept badly, but unsure why. In theory it should have been nice to have his own space, to know he could return to his regular routine for a few hours. There was an element of that, but he was also aware of a sense that something was missing over his solitary bowl of cereal. Or someone.

Ridiculous.

Yet that afternoon when his phone buzzed and Ava's name flashed on the screen he felt a sense of anticipation as he snatched it up.

'Hey.'

'Hey. My mum called. She'd like to meet you.'

'Any particular reason?'

'I'm not sure.' Her voice was guarded. 'But it's probably better to go and see—we don't want any surprises. I thought we could go on to dinner after. I've booked us a table at

Muscat—it's showy but not too showy. We've had a lot of hits on my social media post and there is a definite level of interest.'

'Brilliant.'

'So how about I pick you up at four?'

'Sounds good.' Liam disconnected, aware of a sense of bitter curiosity about the woman he was soon to meet. Karen Casseveti, formerly Lady Karen Hales. The woman who had taken James Casseveti from his first family and thrown her wealth and position behind him, enabled him to set up Dolci, start the Casseveti fairy tale that had picked up pace in direct proportion to the Rourke family decline.

Liam tamped the feelings down. It was the past, over and done with, and he'd decided to put it aside. Yet by the time he climbed into the passenger seat of Ava's car he was aware of an edginess.

One matched by Ava. As ever she looked incredible, her blonde hair styled in a chic knot on the top of her head, the long-sleeved grey floral dress elegant with a hint of pizzazz. Yet he could see the slight strain in the set of her lips and the tension in her shoulders, though her smile was as flawless as ever as she greeted him.

'All set?' she asked.

'Yes. I'm a little curious and a little wary but I'm good.' He glanced at her. 'You OK?'

'Of course.'

He raised his eyebrows and she gave a small rueful nod of acknowledgment. 'OK. I'm a little wary too. I told you that my mum and I aren't seeing eye to eye at the moment and I'm not really sure how she is going to be.'

Half an hour later they pulled up outside a huge Surrey mansion. The gates opened with majestic splendour and Ava drove her small white electric car onto the expansive gravelled drive.

'It's a family house. My mother inherited it,' Ava explained. 'After Dad died Mum moved here. It's usually looked after by a housekeeper who's been with her since Mum was a child.'

The door was pulled open by a stately looking woman, dressed in severe black, her grey hair pulled back in a bun. She bestowed a tight smile on Ava and graced Liam with a small nod.

'Hello, Ellie.' Ava's smile was wide, but he was sure it was strained. 'How are you?'

'I'm fine, thank you.' Ellie's smile was cold. 'But it's not me you should be worried about. It's your mother.' She pulled the door wider. 'Follow me.'

Once along a spacious corridor, with panelled walls and antique furniture, they entered a vast drawing room that imposed its plush richness. Velvet ruled and there was an indescribable air of wealth and heritage in the Georgian-style furniture and the heavy gold brocade curtains.

'Ava.' A woman stepped forward, a woman who shared Ava's blonde hair, though her colour was discreetly and elegantly aided and cut in a sleek bob. Her make-up was perfect, her figure svelte and stylish, though Liam could see the ravages of grief in the dark circles that couldn't be completely concealed. 'And you must be Liam.' The smile was a blend of welcome and appraisal with a hint of condescension, the blue eyes hooded as she rested her gaze on him.

'Mrs Casseveti. It's a pleasure to meet you.'

'Please, call me Karen. Then sit down and we can discuss the best way forward. Ava told me how you are hoping to use your fake relationship to help save your company and help spin Ava some positive publicity too. I'd like to help.'

'That's great, Mum,' Ava said.

'Yes. And in return perhaps you will feel

more inclined to get rid of the usurpers.' The venom in the last word made him flinch.

'We've been through this.' Ava's voice was firm, but he saw her nails clench into her palms, knew how hard this was for her. 'For a start, the will would be very difficult to overturn and would wipe us out in legal bills.'

'I have said I'll foot the cost.'

'Second, this is what Dad wanted. Luca and Jodi are his children.'

'Luca and Jodi Petrovelli are nothing. They didn't even keep your father's name. They do not deserve to even step into Dolci head-quarters.'

'Perhaps. But they have the right to do so. I think we should make the best of it.'

'How can you be so disloyal? Your father made a mistake and I will not let the Petro-vellis get their grubby hands on James's com-pany.' Karen turned to Liam. 'You are an excellent businessman—you've come from nowhere and achieved a lot. I assume you must have a ruthless streak, a business sense. Show Ava the best way forward. The right way.'

Liam read the signs all too well; the same look had dulled his father's eyes with obses-sion. Quickly he stepped closer to Ava, hoped his body warmth could somehow shield her. 'I will support any decision Ava makes.'

Karen exhaled a long sigh; her eyes glittered with ice. 'Ava, show some family loyalty and together we will take that woman's children down.'

'I won't do that, Mum. I won't overturn Dad's wishes. Please, let's work together to try and make the best of this, do what is best for Dolci.'

Karen shook her head, emitted a sigh that gusted disappointment and anger.

But Ava persevered. 'Dolci is in trouble, will stay in trouble until we can get certainty and public confidence. Getting mired in a lengthy legal wrangle won't help.'

The words fell into Karen Casseveti's chasm of resentment. 'Just leave. Come back when you are ready to fix the mess you made. If you had been a better daughter, then your father would not have done this.'

Liam's heart ached for her as he saw the pain in Ava's eyes, the quickly concealed flinch.

'Perhaps that is true,' she said quietly. 'But at least I was given a chance to try to be a good daughter. They weren't given a chance to be anything, not even a peripheral part of his life.' She moved forward, approached her mother. 'I know how betrayed you feel, but this was Dad's fault, not Luca's or Jodi's.'

For a moment Liam wondered if Ava had got through but Karen shook her head. 'I cannot believe you would take their side over me. Please leave now.'

Ava hesitated and then nodded. 'I'll call you later.'

She headed towards the door and Liam followed, knew there was nothing he could say that would turn Karen. He had spent years trying to mitigate Terry Rourke's bitterness to no avail, sensed that Karen's hostility ran equally deep. But at least Terry Rourke hadn't blamed his son, hadn't directed his anger against Liam.

Sensing Ava didn't want to talk, he remained silent as she started the car and began the journey back to London, broke silence only when they were on the outskirts, had stopped to recharge Ava's electric VW. 'Are you sure you still want to go out for dinner?' He knew how much Karen Casseveti's words must have hurt Ava, but saw her expression close down into neutrality, knew she wouldn't talk about it.

'I'm sure. If we don't turn up that's the exact wrong message to send out. It won't help you. Or me.'

After that she adroitly changed the subject, manufactured small talk for the remainder of their journey, until they pulled up in the vicinity of the exclusive restaurant.

Ava focused on the click of her heels on the pavement, the cold February air that permeated the wool of her navy-blue button-down coat. Tried to push down and freeze the negativity and doubts swirled up by her mother. Allowed herself an awareness of Liam's strength and warmth, knew she needed to channel that to play the role of adoring and adored girlfriend, to cast the spell of an illusory love for the public eye to behold.

Because she was going to make this charade work, at least achieve something to help her embattled company. And so she entered the glitz and glamour of the star-studded restaurant with confidence in her walk and in her smile. Chose her food with care—there was no way Ava Casseveti would be snapped with spinach in her teeth, or a food stain on her dress.

When the drinks arrived she raised her sparkling water, aware that many of their fellow diners were watching. 'Cheers,' she said.

'Cheers,' he answered. 'Thank you for seeing this through.'

'No problem. My mother thought this charade a good idea and she knows what she is talking about. So this dinner is important.'

'Just because she knows about spin doesn't mean she knows everything. When someone is obsessed by bitterness their perspective is skewed. Looking back now, I know my father's was. I think your mother's is too. She didn't mean what she said about it being your fault. About you being a better daughter.'

The echo of her mother's words stung. 'Unfortunately the only person who would know that is my dad so I'll never know for sure. But as you said you're dealt the cards you're dealt in life.'

'Yes. Now it's up to you how to play the hand. Seems to me you've got a tricky one. Maybe I can help. Maybe talking about it will help.'

'I don't want to talk about my mother.'

'I meant help with Dolci. In my ruthless businessman role.'

'You want to help me rescue Dolci?'

'Yes. You don't deserve to be in this position. I wouldn't have lifted a finger for your dad but I'd like to help you.'

'I appreciate that.' And she did. 'But there is nothing you can do. I am caught between a rock and a hard place. My mother wants me to overturn the will, work to oust Luca and Jodi. Luca and Jodi are refusing to engage so I don't even know what they want. My dad seemed to think we would all miraculously become a happy family.'

'What about what you want?'

Ava paused, fork halfway to her mouth. 'Me? I'd like... I'd like us all to sit down and talk. But I'd also like world peace—neither is very likely.'

That pulled a smile from him. 'I admit it's hard to see your mother shaking hands with the usurpers. Right now. So maybe that needs to be your long-term goal. You need to think about what you *can* control now. Focus on a short-term goal, an obstacle you can overcome.'

Ava sat for a moment, tasted the succulent flavour of the perfectly cooked lamb and thought about his words. 'I'd like to show the world that I am capable, or at least more capable than they think I am. That my ideas could work.'

'Then pick an idea and do it. Your way.'

Easy to say—she wasn't sure she knew what 'her' way was. 'That's what you would do, but that's because you know what you're doing.'

Liam paused. 'No, I don't. Not always. I

don't want to ruin my image but I certainly
made my share of mistakes.'

'You did?'

'Yes. There was the time I nearly landed
us with a lawsuit when I let myself get distracted and riled during a security assign-
ment. The police tried to arrest me whilst
someone tried to attack the guy I was meant
to be protecting.'

'What happened?'

'I knocked the police officer out so I could
protect the client. It eventually worked out
but it nearly didn't. And another person may
have handled it differently, figured out a less
violent way. But sometimes you have to do it
your way, take a stand, act on your own instincts, take a risk.'

'Maybe I am too risk averse. All I see is
the worst-case scenario.'

Liam shook his head. 'I don't think it's
that.'

'Then what do you think it is?'

He hesitated and she gestured. 'It's fine. Hit
me with it.' She genuinely wanted his opinion, wondered how it had come to matter to
her so much in such a short space of time.

'Right. I think you're too worried about
everyone else. You want to please your father
and your mother and the press and your staff

and you've lost sight of you. That's what I told you from the start. Make the company yours. Show everyone you can do this—if implementing a new green policy is problematic, do something smaller first. But do something.'

Ava swirled her water thoughtfully, pushed her plate away, her mind racing. 'OK. So I need to do something to win their respect. I know what would help—I just have no idea how to do it.'

'Tell me.'

'My dad was about to close a deal with Leonardo Brunetti—he owns a chain of upmarket Italian emporium-type supermarkets. Since my father's death he's been prevaricating and now he's on the verge of pulling out. He's citing the uncertainty of Dolci's future and my inexperience. I can't help feeling that if Luca approached him he'd be fine.'

Liam could hear the bitterness in her voice. 'Because he's a man.'

'Yes, partly, but mostly because Luca has set up his own company, made a success off his own bat.'

'Then how about approaching Luca? You could go to see Leonardo Brunetti together, pitch for the deal.'

'No.' Ava needed to prove to everyone, including Luca, that she could do this herself.

'I need something different. I've done everything I can think of to win Leonardo Brunetti over. Short of giving him the damn products. I have written reports, costed spreadsheets, put together a presentation on why Dolci products are great. But I can't be my father and I can't pretend that Dolci isn't having leadership issues.'

'No, but you can be yourself. Stop apologising for your past and your father. You are a successful woman in your own right.'

'It doesn't feel like that.'

'Then fake it. Like you fake your smile.'

Ava stared at him—why on earth hadn't she thought of that herself? 'You're a genius. Fake it till you make it,' she said. 'I'm good at that.'

There was a heartbeat of silence as the words lingered in the air and the atmosphere changed. Liam leaned forward, raised an eyebrow. 'Really?' he said, his word a long drawl, a teasing glint in his cobalt eyes. 'Interesting.'

Heat crept over her face. 'I wasn't talking about…that.'

'Talking about what?' He maintained a tone of mock innocence but couldn't hold back a grin.

'I wasn't talking about sex,' she muttered.

'I meant that it's like modelling—sometimes you have to act, fake a smile and you keep doing it until it looks real and...then sometimes you find yourself genuinely...'

'Making it?' he offered helpfully.

'Yes.' Against her will she did smile. 'I need to stop digging this hole until it's so deep there's no way I'm getting out of it.'

'It's fine. I'll help you out. Any time.' He wriggled his eyebrows and she chuckled, then he joined in and it was as though they couldn't stop, the laughter an incredible and welcome release from all the pent-up tension and emotion.

'I needed that,' Ava said eventually.

'So did I.'

'Thank you for listening. It's really helped. I feel like I can think more clearly. And you're right. I need to jump off the treadmill because it isn't working. It's as though I'm running as hard as I can to maintain a status quo that can no longer exist.' So she needed a new Ava Casseveti—a new persona. Needed to do something different, eye-catching... 'I've got it!'

'Tell me.'

There it was again, the deep voice, the genuine interest that seemed to caress her skin.

'A fundraiser. A glamorous, glitzy fundraiser. I'll call in some markers in the showbiz world. I'll ask the Brunettis, I'll ask the staff, I'll use my aristocratic connections. Raise shedloads of money for charity. If Dolci goes under at least I'll have done something good that I believe in.'

'That's a brilliant idea.'

'You really think so?'

'Really.'

'So how about we do it together? It would give us something to focus on. We could promote it together, organise it together as a "couple".' And with any luck they could somehow transform all the sexual tension into an energy to create an amazing event. 'You can ask your clients and Ray Beaumont.'

He smiled. 'It's a great idea. Let's do it. First things first. What shall we fundraise for? What is a cause that means a lot to you?'

'I want to raise money for disaster victims and raise awareness about climate change. Given how many natural disasters there have been recently, fires, tornadoes and the devastation caused, I'd like to help.'

'Agreed.'

Sudden excitement fizzed in her, not only for the project, but because Liam hadn't dismissed her idea. Instead he'd encouraged it and she couldn't help but beam at him. And as she did her gaze took him in: the swell of muscle in his upper arm, the sheer masculine beauty of his strong, capable hands, the... Stop!

From now on it needed to be venues, ticket prices, food and canapés all the way. However hard that was going to be.

CHAPTER THIRTEEN

A week later

LIAM DISCONNECTED FROM the call and found himself whistling. This was all coming together. His relationship with Ava had definitely garnered a positive response from clients. He hadn't been so crass as to highlight it to anyone, but there had certainly been sufficient press interest and, of course, the invitations to the fundraiser clinched it.

Rita popped her head round the door. 'You sound happy.'

'I am. That was Ray Beaumont on the phone, accepting the invite. That has to be a good sign that we are back on a level playing field.'

'That is excellent.' Rita glanced at him. 'Is that the only reason you're happy?'

'Of course.'

Rita raised her eyebrow. 'Don't let Ava hear

you say that. I saw the photos of both of you at Lady Mannering's ball yesterday. Mixing with aristocracy and celebrities—you both looked very happy. I'm glad for you, Liam.'

'Yes.' Rita's words took the whistle from his lips, a reminder that all of this was a campaign. A successful one but one that presented an illusion to the world. The smiles for the camera, practised and fake. At the end of each evening he dropped Ava home, made plans for the next day and discussed the fundraiser before heading home. 'Thank you,' he added.

'I came to tell you that Ava called whilst you were on the phone. She is on her way over.'

Liam frowned. They had no plans for today, which could mean a glitch.

Five minutes later Rita ushered Ava in and, with a small finger-wave, departed.

'Is everything OK?'

'Yes and no.' Ava looked perturbed and more than a touch annoyed. 'Emily called me.' Ava's best friend. 'Apparently a reporter called her, one of the more scurrilous ones, asking questions, about our "authenticity".'

'Meaning?'

'She's noticed that we don't seem to stay over at each other's houses.' Ava grimaced.

'I'm sorry, Liam. That is a huge detail and I overlooked it.'

'That's OK.' In truth he knew why she had, why they both had. Neither of them wanted to risk the intimacy of a 'sleepover'. 'So did I. The important thing now is damage limitation.'

'Yup. I thought maybe I could stay over at your house at the weekend? My flat only has one bedroom so... You'd need to sleep on the sofa.'

'That's fine. But to make a bit more of a splash, shall we go away for a night? Then return to my place? You look like you could do with a break.' She looked tired, he noticed with a flash of guilt. The effort of maintaining this charade was perhaps taking its toll. She didn't even like parties, was doing this for him. As she had for Nick. He pushed the guilt down. This was a finite time plan.

'I'm fine. Really.'

But the words didn't ring true and he frowned. 'I'm not buying it. I'll arrange it. Surprise you. I'll pick you up after work tonight. Think how good it will look on social media. And it will hopefully stop this reporter before she gets too close.' He frowned. 'I'm willing to bet that AJ set her on the scent.'

'Then we'd better head her off at the pass.

The night away and staying over are great up to a point, but we need something more... girl next door.' Now she glanced at him. 'We could—' She broke off, a troubled look in her amber eyes.

'Could what?'

She shook her head. 'It occurred to me that we should do some more family things and then I thought I bet Max would love it if we went skating where he works as a volunteer skate guard. But I don't want to use Max and I don't want to raise his hopes that this would be the start of something. If we do it we need to keep it very casual and you should only do it if you are truly willing to engage with him.'

Liam looked at her and for the first time he wondered if Ava could be right. Was it possible that Max wanted a better relationship, any sort of relationship with Liam? The thought was scary but also...tempting? He forced himself to think—the one thing he wouldn't do was risk anyone being hurt, wouldn't raise expectations he couldn't fulfil.

'Let's see if we can think of anything else. You're right. It doesn't feel right to use Max.'

Ava thought for a moment. 'How about I organise something? Your mum says she watches that dance programme on TV. Do you think she'd like to meet one of the contestants? Anna Lise is a mate of mine from my modelling days.'

'She'd love that.'

'I'll sort it out. I'll take your mum out for a drink with Anna Lise.' She looked him straight in the eye. 'That way you don't have to be involved at all. If that's what you prefer.'

He could see challenge and sadness in her eyes, a sadness that reflected his own, that came straight from the part of him that wanted to be in a family unit, to be part of his mum's life, and for a moment he was tempted to go skating, to go for a drink, to…get involved.

Then common sense reasserted itself. Too risky. Involvement was complicated, painful, scary. It would invoke responsibility.

'That's what I prefer.'

The sadness intensified in her eyes and she nodded. 'OK. I'll speak to Anna Lise and your mum.'

'And I'll sort out a weekend getaway.'

Once Ava had gone, Liam sat at his desk, stared at the doorway for a while as guilt niggled him again. There had been shadows in her eyes and he had the feeling he'd put them there. Dammit! The least he could do was find the perfect getaway, give Ava a chance to recharge and maybe bring a genuine smile to her face.

* * *

By Friday evening Liam was confident he'd achieved his aim, sure that he'd found the perfect place to chase away the shadows from Ava's eyes. He looked sideways at Ava, pleased to see that she was fast asleep, had been since they started the journey.

He pulled to a stop and anticipation buzzed inside him as she stirred. For a moment sleep-clouded eyes dreamily stared at him and he saw something there, an elusive happiness that warmed something in him. The idea that someone could look at him like that triggered a strange sense of lightness.

Then Ava blinked and the look was gone, so ephemeral that he might well have imagined it. Knew he should hope he had.

'Here we are.'

As she took in the scene her amber eyes lit up and a sudden shaft of happiness touched him. 'It's like a tree house,' she said as she gazed at the wooden structure on stilts, whose roof peaked and nestled in the boughs of the trees.

'A tree house with five-star luxury guaranteed. Let's go check it out.' His lips were up-turned in a grin that he suspected held a hint of goofiness and he didn't care. Just once he would give in to this unfamiliar sense of exhilaration, the precarious lightness of being.

He opened her car door and they headed to the stairs that led to the edifice, climbed the planks to the wooden door. Once inside they both paused on the threshold and gazed at the airy, sumptuous interior.

'I love it.' Ava gestured towards the spiral staircase that twisted up from the centre of the room, then at the iron wood-burning stove, replete with logs. She walked over to the window and glanced out at the view. 'It's beautiful. Sprawling fields, and a farm.'

Over to one side a simple Shaker-style kitchenette boasted a state-of-the-art oven and gleaming wooden worktops overhung with copper pans suspended on hooks. A separate section had been designated the dining area, complete with an oak dining table and matching chairs, whilst the other side of the spacious floor was the lounge with a soft, squishy sofa and a large television.

Another door led to a small second bedroom with twin beds. 'I'll have this one,' Ava said firmly.

'Let's look upstairs.' They climbed up the spiral stairs complete with pretty wrought-iron balustrade and into the master bedroom. 'Wow.' This room was magical; it would feel like sleeping nestled in the treetops. Triangular skylights showcased the clear late afternoon skies touched with the setting sun. And the enormous bed filled nearly all available space.

In tacit consent they both beat a hasty retreat back down the stairs into the lounge.

'Why don't I get the stove going?' Liam suggested.

'Good plan. I'll just pop to the bathroom and then I'll check the supplies.'

As the logs caught flame and the flicker of firelight danced across the sheepskin rug Ava returned with a platter. 'There are cold meats and English cheese and freshly baked bread and organic salad. All from the farm. Does that sound OK? We could have an indoor picnic.'

'Perfect.'

Once settled on the sumptuous sheepskin rug, she glanced at him. 'Thanks for finding this. It's perfect.'

'For social media posts?'

'Yes, but that's not what I meant. It's exactly what I would have picked myself. When you talked about making a splash I thought you might choose somewhere more…public. Where we'd be seen, or snapped, or something.'

Liam shook his head. 'You've done enough

of that. This is more about saying thank you. I know it must be a strain maintaining this charade.'

Now the sweetness of her smile trickled warmth over his chest. 'It's not the charade. Truly. And remember, this is benefiting me as well. At work everyone is really getting behind the fundraiser.'

'Then what is the matter? If it's not the charade?'

'It doesn't matter.'

'Yes. It does. Tell me.'

She hesitated, bought time by cutting a wedge of the tart farmhouse cheddar. 'I'm being silly. It's the same old story but this has made me feel…sad.' She tugged her phone out of her jeans pocket. 'I emailed Luca and Jodi about the fundraiser and today I finally got a reply. Here you go.'

She scrolled down and handed him the phone.

Dear Ms Casseveti

Mr Petrovelli has asked me to inform you of the following:

He is more than happy to endorse and support the fundraiser—please feel free to organise as you wish.

Unfortunately neither he nor Ms Petrovelli will be able to attend.

Liam handed the phone back as Ava sighed. 'It's so cold and formal. I mean, who would think we are related? I get that after what happened we aren't a family, but surely he could answer me himself. It just makes me feel sad.'

He got that. Yet… 'Of course it does, but I do wonder what's going on. Luca is a businessman, a successful one at that—his attitude to Dolci doesn't make sense.'

'Clearly his feelings about what my father did outweigh business sense. This is personal.'

Liam shook his head. 'If Luca was truly vindictive he would have refused to endorse anything. It's formal, yes, but it's not nasty. It could be there is something else at play here that we don't know about.'

'Do you really think so?'

'I think it's possible.'

Ava scooped a spoon of chutney and added it to her plate. 'That hadn't occurred to me, but actually you have a point. It is all rather odd.' Now she smiled and he felt a small sense of satisfaction as she relaxed slightly. 'Thank you for your sense of perspective—I seem to have mislaid mine somewhere.'

As she finished speaking her phone rang and she glanced at the screen. 'Sorry, I'll have to take it. It's my lawyer.'

'Go ahead.'

'Vince. Hi.' He watched as her face creased into a frown of perplexity, then he rose to go and open some wine, returned with two glasses. 'She wants to do what? Can she do that?' She listened some more and then, 'Thank you for letting me know.'

She dropped the phone on the floor and shook her head. He could see a gamut of emotions chase across her face. Disbelief, anger and a weariness that made his heart ache.

'What's happened?'

'It turns out that Mum has decided to try and overturn the will herself—she wants to oust us all and try and get control of Dolci for herself.'

'Do you want to go and see her? Now? Talk to her?'

Ava shook her head and he could see tears glistening in her eyes. 'There's no point. There's nothing I can do to stop this and I'm not even sure I want to any more. Perhaps I should just hand her my share and leave them all to it.' She placed one hand on her tummy and quickly dashed her other hand against her eyes. 'I am not going to cry.'

For a moment panic threatened to engulf him as his comfort zone was cut from beneath his feet to leave him over an abyss. He didn't know how to deal with situations like this—never had, never would. But then, from somewhere, instinct came to his rescue with the inherent visceral knowledge that he had to do something to ease her pain.

Rising, he moved over, dropped down next to her. 'It's OK to cry. Come here.' It was so natural to pull her into his arms, breathe in the scent of her shampoo and offer what comfort and understanding he could. He heard the small hiccough and then the tears did come, gentle at first and then a torrent. He rubbed her back, made soothing sounds, held her close until finally she pulled away, swiped at her eyes.

'I'm sorry.' She opened her bag and pulled out a packet of tissues, blew her nose. 'I can only imagine what I look like. I doubt even my waterproof mascara can hold up to that.'

'You look beautiful.' The words were out before he could stop them and she shook her head.

'I look a blotchy, splotchy mess. But I do feel better. Even though I still have no idea what to do about it.'

'Maybe talk to your mum, tell her that this

will be worse for Dolci. I very much doubt she stands a chance legally, but it could take years for it to go through the courts.'

'It won't make a difference. As you said— she is obsessed. She was obsessed when Dad was alive and she is still obsessed now.' Ava's voice was weary. 'All her life she's been terrified Dad would leave her. Leave us. Go back to his first wife, his first family. All her life she strove to be the perfect wife, to hold and bind him to her.' She shook her head, sipped her wine as she stared into the distance.

'And all your life you tried to be the perfect daughter.'

'Yes. We were an alliance, I guess. I can remember Mum telling me how dangerous Luca and Jodi were. I used to picture them lurking round every corner. I worried they'd kidnap my dad. Then I started to worry that I wouldn't be enough to keep him.'

Liam tried to imagine the burden of anxiety, could almost picture a wide-eyed child Ava, small hands clenched into determined fists, as so many things became clear to him. Her perfect smile, the way Ava always looked flawless, knew how to act whatever part was required of her, the way she still wanted to try and please everyone. The immense pressure she put on herself to do what was right. 'That should never have felt like your responsibility.'

'No.' She looked at him. 'But life doesn't always work like that, does it? It should never have felt your responsibility to try to get your father back on track. Your mother's happiness was never your weight to bear.'

'That's different. My mother had a chance of happiness that she gave up because of my actions and my existence.'

Ava shook her head. 'No, your parents' marriage and how it worked out was not down to you. They chose to have a child and actually it's OK for a parent to put their child first, to be responsible for their happiness. Your mum did the right thing and I am sure it is a decision she would make again.'

'Whereas your mum didn't put your happiness first.' The idea and its ramifications, the possibility that his mum had done what any mother would do, edged into his consciousness, only to be rebutted as he focused on Ava.

Ava shook her head. 'Nothing is as clear-cut as that. My father was her everything, and she believed I should feel the same way, that my happiness was also bound to him. She only had a child because she thought it would ensure my dad stayed.'

Liam shifted closer to her and draped his arm over her shoulders, as if he could belatedly shield her from the machinations of her parents. He loathed the idea that Ava had been a pawn in some obsessive game even as he struggled to understand it. 'But I thought your parents' marriage was a fairy tale.'

Ava shook his head. 'I told you my mother was the Queen of Spin. I believe the real story is he left his first family because my mother had the wealth and connections that would enable him to start Dolci.'

'He could have got a bank loan.'

'He took the easy option. I think my mother dazzled him. She told me it was love at first sight, that once she saw him she had to have him. And after that she had to keep him.'

As if he were some sort of prize specimen. 'Do you think he loved her?'

'I don't know.' Ava lifted her slim shoulders. 'Define love. Perhaps he thought the pay-off was worth it—he gained celebrity, wealth, his business, a beautiful wife who worshipped the ground he walked on. But he lived in a gilded cage with a replacement family. And I don't think we truly lived up to the original, however much he tried to convince himself we did.'

His heart tore as he listened to her, imagined how it must have felt to always feel second best to one parent and a tool to the other. 'But he did love you.'

'Yes, he did. I helped him atone for his past.'

'Ava, I'm sorry. All of that is too much for one person to carry.' Only she had carried it and carried it without complaint. More than that, she hadn't let it blight her life.

'No. I don't want your pity.' She shifted to face him and the flicker of the firelight dappled her blonde hair, illuminated the classic beauty of her face, emphasised its strength and character. 'I've had a good life. I've never wanted for any material thing and my father did love me. We had good times together. Good family times. And my parents were happy in their own way. Their life was hardly full of hardship. I have friends, a job I love, if I could only figure out how to do it.'

'I'm not pitying you.' He needed her to believe that, understood exactly what she meant. 'I am full of admiration for you and the way you have dealt with everything life has thrown at you. Not just dealt with it— you've thrived.'

Now their gazes locked and he couldn't help it, she was so close, so beautiful, he leant forward and lightly brushed his lips against hers and an intensity of sweetness flooded him, as if he were afloat in sensory joy. He deepened the kiss, and her arms looped round his neck, her body pressed against his, and now the background faded and there was nothing except Ava. But this time he knew a kiss couldn't be enough, for either of them, could feel her need, her yearning, match his. He craved the taste of her skin, to touch, caress and revel in her body. To glide his hand over the satin sheen of her bare skin.

Her hand slid under the soft cotton of his shirt and he heard his own groan as she placed it over the beat of his heart.

'Ava.' Her name was a whisper, a question, and she pulled away slightly.

Placed a finger against his lips. 'Shh. I want this, Liam. To lose myself in this, forget the world and reality and just feel.'

Now a muffled alarm rang in his head, trying to tell him, warn him, and he didn't want to listen, dammit. This was right, beautiful, wonderful... 'I want you,' she said.

'And I want you.'

'Then what are we waiting for?' Her voice was breathless, caught on a half-laugh, half-gasp of desire.

Then he remembered that he hadn't prepared for this moment, hadn't intended it.

As if she read his mind she pressed close to him. 'Don't worry. Five-star service includes a discreet stash of condoms. I happened to find them earlier when I went to the loo.'

Relief swathed him. 'Then what *are* we waiting for?' Rising, he tugged her up with him and they climbed the spiral stairs, entered the magical, beautiful bedroom and he tumbled her back onto the bed, under the canopy of the stars.

CHAPTER FOURTEEN

THE NEXT MORNING Ava opened her eyes, saw the twist and tumble of the sheet, felt colour heat her checks as she saw her clothes strewn haphazardly on the floor. Closed her eyes for a moment and allowed herself to savour the memories of the previous hours: the heat, the passion, the laughter and the joy as their bodies intertwined, discovered each other. Explored, touched, gave and received such intense pleasure.

But where was Liam? And, more to the point, what now?

For a second Ava was tempted to lie back and hide under the duvet, but before she could do anything Liam popped his head round the door.

'Morning, sleepy head. I've got breakfast on the go. A full English awaits, all local produce, all fresh and all delicious.'

'I'll be right down. Give me ten minutes.'

Ten minutes to figure this out. Lord knew she didn't, couldn't, regret the night just gone, but she also knew it shouldn't have happened. Her mind whirred, told her that it was impossible to analyse this situation until she could gauge what Liam thought.

She had no idea how he felt—all she knew was his preference for one-night stands and no emotional involvement. Was that what last night had been? For Liam that was all it could be—the only way he could reconcile it with his feelings for Jess. Jess—would he be thinking of her now? Had he been thinking of her last night? No, she wouldn't believe that—couldn't believe it.

Shoving aside the whisper of doubt, she swung her legs out of bed, her mind analysing what to wear, how to project the right persona—cool, casual, the sort of modern mature woman who could separate sex from emotion. She settled for jeans and a long cream knitted jumper. Kept her hair loose and her make-up minimal.

As she entered the kitchen he smiled, but his cobalt eyes held caution even though his tone was light. 'Perfect timing.'

'It looks delicious. Thank you.' Yet right now the idea of food made her tummy ache and loop as she watched Liam. She could almost see the barricade he had put up. Gone was the man who had taken her to such heights mere hours ago, the man who had held her with such tenderness and stoked her to such passion. For a moment Ava wondered if the whole night had been a series of fevered dreams. 'We need to talk.'

'Yes.' Wariness played over his face, but it was more than that—she could see regret, apprehension, and that made hurt twist inside her.

'Last night was…wonderful and I don't regret it one bit.' His shoulders relaxed slightly and the worry made a small retreat in his cobalt eyes and gave her the impetus to continue. 'And I hope you don't either.'

His gaze met hers. 'I don't regret it.'

But she could see shadows in his eyes, and she wondered what he was thinking. Of Jess? Did this feel like a betrayal of his wife? 'I'm not sure that's true,' she said, careful to keep her voice gentle. 'I know you prefer one-night stands with women you don't know.'

Three strides and he had moved round the breakfast bar, was standing in front of her. 'Look at me.' Oh, so gently he raised a hand and placed a finger under her chin, tipping it up so she met his gaze. 'I swear last night was magical. I don't even know how to put it into words…and I don't regret it. But it wasn't planned or intended and I'm worried I took advantage of you. You were upset and you are still grieving and…'

Ava saw the sincerity in his eyes, and a thrill shot through her that Liam too had found the night magical. 'You didn't take advantage of me at all. I wanted last night.'

'I sense a but…'

He was right. Because whilst she did believe Liam's concern that he had taken advantage of her was legitimate, she could still see that he was haunted. 'But I know you must be feeling something about Jess.'

His flinch was almost imperceptible though his gaze stayed locked on hers. 'This isn't about Jess, this is about you.'

Leave it at that, Ava. But she couldn't. 'It's also about you and what you feel. Do you feel guilty?'

There was a fraction of a heartbeat before he answered and before he could Ava raised a hand. 'I'm sorry. I shouldn't have asked that.' Wished, oh, so much that she hadn't, but it was too late to swallow the question. 'Of course you feel guilt. You loved her. So a magical night with someone else must feel like a betrayal.' That knowledge hurt—too reminiscent of a lifelong awareness that, by being with his second family, her father was betraying his first family. But that wasn't Liam's fault. 'I'm sorry.'

'Ava.' His voice was hoarse. 'I—'

'It's OK. Last night took us both by surprise. We'll put it behind us and—'

He shook his head. 'Stop. I need to tell you something. I can't let you believe this any more.'

'I don't understand.'

He rubbed a hand over his face, inhaled deeply. 'My marriage wasn't the idyll you believe it to be.' Ava saw his pain, but she also sensed he didn't want comfort or interruption. He simply needed to get the words out. 'I met Jess when I was young and grieving. She was there and I mistook liking and need for love. When she thought she was pregnant I married her, even though I knew by then I didn't love her. It turned out she wasn't pregnant but by then the knot was tied. I'd made my vows and I wanted to stand by them.'

As his mother had done.

'I believed that I could make myself love her, force the emotion into being. Believed her love would somehow force me to do the right thing and love her back. It didn't work like that. The worst of it was that Jess still loved me and I was too much of a coward to admit I didn't. So I let her waste her life on me.'

'No!' The denial pulled from her as her heart turned at his words. At the pressure he'd piled onto himself, born of his own hopes and wishes that his parents would be happy together, would make their marriage work. Born of his belief that a person should never renege on a promise. After all, his father had been betrayed by a man who had done just that. So his word was his bond. Liam would have been incapable of breaking his marriage vows and as long as Jess had wanted to stay he would always have done his best. 'You did what you thought was right. You didn't want to hurt Jess.'

'But if I had, if I had been more honest, then perhaps she would have found real happiness.'

'It doesn't work like that. You can't second-guess something you can't change. Jess may have been miserable without you and…' she kept her voice gentle '… Jess had choices too. She chose to stay in your marriage as well. Neither of you could have known of the tragedy in store.'

'But she is the one who paid the biggest price.'

'Yes. But that is no fault of yours.' But she

knew to Liam it felt as if it was, knew that he blamed himself for the failure of his marriage, the might-have-beens and what-ifs. She moved closer to him. 'All the worst-case scenarios. You don't really know them. If you'd left Jess she may have ended up more unhappy, if your mother had left your father she and John may not have worked out. It all may have been worse.'

'You're right. But it all may have been better. I'll never know. Because I can't change the past. But I can at least control my present and my future.'

And that was why he'd never risk a relationship or love again. Even as she understood that, the knowledge sent a sudden stab of bleakness through her, one she refused to give in to. Especially when she could see the demons that rode his shoulder, saw the haunted depths of his cobalt eyes.

'You're right. The past can't be changed and we don't know the repercussions if we could. We can imagine all the what ifs but we can't truly know. But we can make choices in the here and now.' And she moved closer to him, looped her arms around his waist, stretched up on tiptoe and brushed her lips against his. 'I think we should choose to enjoy our magic for a few weeks, forget the past and focus on the present.'

For a moment his body remained taut with a hard edge of tension and then slowly she felt him relax, the soft expel of breath, the release of tightness as he gathered her close.

'Are you sure it's what you want?'

'I'm sure.' And she was, knew that, whatever happened next, this was the right decision, the start of a heady few weeks that she would always remember. 'So how about we postpone breakfast and head back to bed?' And with a provocative look she sashayed to the door in her best model walk, stood in the doorway and in one fluid move unzipped her dress and let it pool to the ground, stepped over the material and continued to walk. She heard his sharp intake of breath, shivered in anticipation as she sensed his presence mere centimetres behind her, felt the brand of his hand on the small of her back as they walked towards the stairs.

A week later—the night of the fundraiser

Ava checked her to-do list yet again, told her twitching nerves that she had everything under control. She looked round the plush hotel room, tried to ground herself, smiled as Liam emerged from the shower.

'Need some distraction?'

'You'll do nicely.' It still seemed surreal to Ava that for now she had unlimited, unfettered access to Liam's sheer gorgeousness. That she had an intimate knowledge of the swell of every muscle, the sweep of his spine, the crook of his arm where she fell asleep each night.

His gaze devoured her with equal interest. 'Shame you're already in the dress,' he said.

For a moment she contemplated shimmying straight out of it but a glance at the clock told her that was not a good idea. She needed to look poised, perfect, every hair in place, make-up pristine… 'Later, I promise I won't be.'

'I'll hold you to that.' The deep rumble of his voice sent a shiver down her spine and she marvelled at her body's response to him. 'You look stunning and I promise you've got this. It will be the event of the year. You've done a superb job.'

'We've done a superb job.'

'Nope. Own this. It's yours. You've brought flair and style and passion to it. The vegan canapés, the way you haven't used plastics, the fact sheets and talking points dotted around the function room—it all shows you believe in the cause you are raising money for.'

Ava smiled at him, touched by the sincerity in his voice. 'Thank you.'

'They'll enjoy the champagne, the food, the music and the company and having their awareness raised in a subtle manner that encourages them to part with their money at the auction.' He moved away and dropped the towel, pulled on boxers and a pair of tuxedo pants and for a moment she simply stared, caught anew by his unselfconscious nakedness. This could never get old.

Literally, she reminded herself. Because in a few weeks they would part ways, the fun would be over. In which case it made sense to make the most of it now, because discovering her body's capacity for Liam was a learning curve and she was enjoying every inch of the climb. He adjusted his cufflinks and a sudden pang hit her. It was so... intimate, so domestic despite the glamour, and it made her heart do a funny little hop, skip and a jump.

Whoa. Just sex and fun, remember?

And now she needed to focus on the evening ahead.

'Speaking of the auction.'

She sensed the hesitation in Liam's voice.
'Yes?'

'There's a last-minute addition to the donations. From Luca.'

'Luca?'

'I contacted him to ask. I didn't tell you because I didn't want to get your hopes up. Especially when I didn't hear back. But then earlier today an item arrived. A painting by an Italian artist. And an email message.'

He picked up his phone and showed her.

Dear Liam
I have dispatched a donation for the auction. I wish you and Ava luck in raising money for this excellent cause.
Best wishes
Luca Petrovelli

Ava stared at it for a long moment and the smallest tendril of hope unfurled. It wasn't gushing, it was bland, but it wasn't unfriendly and it wasn't vindictive. Happiness brought an extra spring to her step as she moved towards Liam and wrapped her arms around him.

'Thank you, Liam. That was good of you.' Kind. Thoughtful. Caring. Stop…leave it there. Stepping back, she turned to the mirror, warned herself to rein in emotion. One last glance at her reflection, a small adjustment to the folds of the dress, one final swipe of lipstick. 'Ready to go.'

'Ready to go.' He smiled at her and took her hand in his. 'So we meet and greet each guest at the door, then we mingle, then we eat, then we auction.'

'That's the plan.'

'Then we thank everyone, say goodbye and come up here, where there will be champagne on ice waiting for us.'

A bubble of anticipation brought a smile to her face and she squeezed his hand as they left the room and headed downstairs to greet their guests. Ava cast a last glance of approval at the ballroom of the plush London hotel. Eco-friendly rose petals sprinkled the tables, the chairs were bedecked with bows and silver streamers looped and swirled from the ornate vaulted ceilings. Waiting staff were poised to circulate with glasses of champagne and soft drinks and plates of canapés.

'Here we go,' Liam murmured, and they stepped forward to greet their first guests. Twenty minutes later a compact grey-haired man barrelled in, a man with an aura of power. He had a woman on his arm, a woman who had decided to go grey naturally and was comfortable with her decision. As well she might be, Ava thought. Because she was beautiful, with classic features that endured with age.

'Hello, Ray. I'm so glad you could make it.' Liam turned to Ava. 'Ava, this is Ray Beaumont.'

Ray Beaumont. The man who led Beaumont Industries, the man whose business Liam wanted to win. The contract he was in danger of losing to AJ Mason.

The man held his hand out. 'Liam. Ava. Thanks for the invite. This is my wife of thirty years, Sophia.'

The woman gave a soft laugh. 'Honestly, Ray, you sound like you've been counting.'

'I have, my love. And every year I feel more thankful.'

There was obvious affection in the banter and Ava instantly suppressed a pang of what she really hoped wasn't envy. Reminded herself that this was a moment in their married life that might not even be real. Perhaps they stayed together because a divorce would be too expensive.

Reminding herself of her role, she smiled but judged it best not to overdo it. Ray Beaumont was a shrewd businessman. His small grey eyes looked twinkly enough but she sensed the assessment and matched it with a friendly but non-gushy smile of her own.

Once the couple had walked off she murmured to Liam, 'Do you want to go speak with him?'

'Nope. This is about fundraising for a good cause and allowing our guests to network, not about trying to secure a contract. In truth, when I think about the victims we are raising money for my business concerns seem petty.'

The words hit home as she acknowledged the simple truth of them and knowing that made the arrival of Leonardo Brunetti easy to deal with. Because this event wasn't about business—it was about fundraising. That was all that mattered here. There would be time enough for deals in the future. And so she greeted Leonardo and his wife the same way she had greeted everyone else and soon after that she and Liam joined the swirling throng of people.

Ava talked, smiled, chatted, mingled and all the while she was aware of Liam's presence, the calm way he dealt with any problems, the quiet behind-the-scenes preparations for the auction. All done without drama or fuss.

They had agreed to auction off the items

together, taking it in turns, and Ava stepped up to the podium first, faltered as she suddenly spotted her mother at a table, realised Karen Casseveti must have slipped in late. Liam followed her gaze and stepped closer to her. 'Don't let her spook you. This is your show. Not hers.'

Liam was right. It was time to show her mum that Ava too could put on a show, organise an event for a good cause other than the Casseveti brand. If her mother did decide to bring down the edifice then this would be Ava's grand finale.

She brought the gavel down.

'Guests. Liam and I would like to thank you for attending and soon we hope to be thanking you for digging deep and paying for these amazing items so generously donated to raise money for what I hope you agree is a worthy cause. I'm up first and I'll be auctioning off a dress donated by my good friend and fellow model Anna Lise. Next up will be the camera used to photograph Hollywood icons donated by my wonderful friend and a fashion photographer herself, Emily Khatri. Unfortunately Emily can't be here tonight but she says, "Bid high!"'

The bidding began with lots of good-natured banter and generosity and by the end of it Ava's face wanted to crack from smiling so much, especially when she spotted Leonardo Brunetti win Luca's donation—and a bit of her wondered if her brother had picked something that he knew Leonardo would like.

When the final bid was made guests began to circulate again and the band struck up. On automatic Ava looked round for Liam, wanted to share her happiness, maybe have a glass of champagne and toast their success. Her eyes scanned the room and then she froze as she saw Karen Casseveti heading straight for Liam. For a mad moment she wanted to throw herself between them. Forced herself to turn away to talk to a guest. It was perfectly natural for them to speak with each other.

CHAPTER FIFTEEN

Liam glanced around the crowded room and a deep satisfaction rolled over him—the event was an undeniable hit and they'd raised a hefty sum for their cause. And he had stood by his decision not to discuss business with Ray Beaumont or any other of his clients. All he'd learnt about the charity had given him undoubted perspective. Honesty compelled him to admit that he still wanted to win the Beaumont contract, still wanted to mash AJ into the dirt, but if he failed he'd handle defeat a little better than he would have before.

'You look thoughtful.'

He turned as Karen Casseveti approached. Today she looked amazing, all ravages of grief hidden, though her dress was a deep sombre black that conveyed a sense of mourning combined with style.

'What a success. You must be proud of yourself.'

'I am. Though most of the credit goes to Ava—your daughter is an exceptional fund raiser.'

'Yes.' Karen's smile held a touch of resignation. 'She had a good teacher. Me. But that isn't what I would like to discuss with you.'

Caution warned him to tread with care. 'Go ahead.'

'I want to propose an alliance between us. I want your help. I want Ava to have what she deserves and that is Dolci. The company is her birthright and she should be the one at the helm. Not the Petrovellis.'

'That isn't what James believed. Or what Ava wants.'

'Tcha. James was a fool when it came to sentiment. I am not and I won't stand by and see Dolci destroyed and my daughter cheated. I want that will overturned. Even if I have to do it myself, then give Ava her rightful birthright.'

'I understand how you feel but it is not up to me. Or you.'

'But you could persuade Ava to see my point of view. My daughter loves you—you could influence her, guide her to do the right thing. It would benefit you both.'

Liam forced his expression to remain neutral even as panic blazed along his synapses and his brain scrambled. 'I think you're forgetting the truth about Ava and me.' He kept his voice low and the words as open to interpretation as possible.

'I am forgetting nothing. I know how this started but, whilst I may not be the world's best mother, I know my daughter. More than that, I recognise love. Ava loves you for real. I can see it in how she looks at you, the way her eyes follow you across the room.'

Liam stared at her, unable to say a word, his entire body frozen as he struggled to command logic to come to his aid. Ava did not love him. She was faking it. *Fake it till you make it.* Oh, God, was that what they had done.

They? Did he love Ava? The thought was too huge to compute. He couldn't have let that happen. Would never again subject himself or another to the vagaries, the complexities, the misery that love engendered. If he had been fool enough to let love slide, glissade under his skin, he had to get rid of it now. Before it took hold.

He saw Karen look at him and a small smile played across her lips. 'Why is this so bad? You and Ava make a great couple. You could do great things together. Like James and I did. You could end up on the board of Dolci—that would have made your father happy, wouldn't it? Your children could end up at the helm. As it should be.'

Liam wanted to shout, wanted to make the words cease. 'I wouldn't use Ava to win Dolci. I built up Rourke Securities on my own and my father would be proud of that.'

'But you are using Ava now. To win a contract.'

Oh, God. She was right. He'd used Ava, manipulated her need to make amends for her father's actions. Had forced her into faking a persona to the world. Just as she'd done all her life. For years she'd played the part of Ava Casseveti, perfect daughter, and now he'd made her play the role of perfect girlfriend, instead of allowing her to be herself. Worse, he'd done it whilst she was grieving and at her most vulnerable.

He pulled himself together. No matter what, he wouldn't be the reason this fundraiser failed, nor would it be because of him that the charade was exposed. He would not bring humiliation onto Ava. 'Mrs Casseveti, I think you have simply underestimated your daughter's acting abilities. In any case, I have no intention of influencing Ava, even if I could. I trust her to make the right decisions for Dolci. Perhaps you should consider supporting Ava and working with her. I know how important you are to her. Maybe it's time for a fresh start?'

Karen Casseveti shook her head. 'It's too late for that. The Petrovellis won't just disappear.'

'No. They won't. But you don't have to remain enemies—maybe you can all have a fresh start. The past can't be changed but you have a choice in the here and now.' Those had been Ava's words and they held good. 'Think about it,' he added.

The older woman said nothing, then unexpectedly she smiled. 'Perhaps I will.'

Liam nodded and with that he turned to find Ava. As he made his way across the room, with a smile and a word for the guests, he told himself Karen had got it wrong. Ava did not love him and he did not love Ava. As he reached her he saw the shade of worry in her amber eyes but before either of them could say anything Leonardo Brunetti approached them. 'I wanted to congratulate you, congratulate you both. This was an excellent event. Did you organise it yourselves?'

'Yes, we did.'

'Can I ask why you did it?'

'I wanted to do something good, Signor Brunetti. As you know, Dolci is in a complicated place and I wanted to achieve something positive. Something that has nothing to do with shares or profit and loss. Something that shows what I want Dolci to become. An ethical, good company. I believe in our products and I'll never skimp on quality but I must make sure we are doing our best for the climate, for future generations. I want to use potato-starch plastic instead of what we use. If we export to Europe—' and now she smiled at him, with a hint of mischief '—then I plan to do it in as environmentally friendly a way as possible. Perhaps start a manufacturing plant in Europe once we have enough interest, though I would also work on keeping our product exclusive. There's a lot to think about.'

'Indeed there is. But it sounds as if you have many ideas. Once I was like that. Now my wife tells me I am too hidebound. She has read all the documents here, she listened to your speech and she says I should stop being so set in my ways, should move with the times. You have done a good job, Ava. Accept an old man's congratulations.'

'Thank you.'

'Now we will take our leave. I will be in touch. And thank your brother for his donation—this is my favourite painter.' An old-fashioned bow and Leonardo Brunetti turned and made his way back to his wife.

After that there was little chance for conversation until all the guests had departed. The whole time Liam ensured he stayed in role, kept the smile on his lips, but for the first time in a long time he knew the smile to be fake. The practised smile that Ava had taught him how to achieve. Then finally the last lingering guest had departed, the final preparations for pick-up of the auction items had been squared away. For a mad second Liam wanted to chase after them, tell them to stay longer, wanted to put off the moment he and Ava would be alone.

The knowledge streaked sadness through him as he remembered how easy, how comfortable, how happy they'd been earlier. The intimacy, the banter, the talk, the anticipation of the night to come. All torn away by Karen Casseveti's words. Words that might hold no truth—yet he couldn't shake the sense of doom, the belief that the worst-case scenario was about to blow up in his face.

'Shall we go up?' Ava came and stood by his side. 'I think we deserve a glass of bubbly to celebrate.' Her tone was bright, strove for their earlier ease, but he could see the strain in her smile.

'Absolutely. This was an incredible success. You should be proud.' He paused. 'And whilst I know this wasn't the purpose, I believe that Leonardo Brunetti will sign on the dotted line.'

'What about Ray Beaumont?'

'I think he will give me a fair shot now and that's all I could ask for.'

Somehow each and every word felt like a prelude to goodbye, to the end he knew had to come.

As they'd talked they'd made their way up the grand staircase with its plush carpet and oak bannisters. He pushed the door open and allowed Ava to enter, careful—oh, so careful—not to touch her even by mistake. Saw the question, the insinuation of doubt and hurt in her eyes as she turned to him. Once inside their room he looked round, wondered that it looked exactly as they'd left it and yet everything seemed different.

Ava stopped, put a hand out to stop him as he headed for the champagne.

'Wait. Tell me what's wrong. What did Mum say?'

Now was the moment. He'd tell her, she'd scoff and they could…could what? Keep going with the charade that was no longer a charade? That was no longer a possibility—

that he knew. Because even if Karen wasn't right the danger was too great. How had he been so blind? Had he really believed they could live together, sleep together, wake up together and it mean nothing?

Yes. He had. Because he was a fool, a man who did not understand how emotions worked. That was how he'd ended up in a marriage he'd had no idea how to navigate.

But this time he knew what to do, knew he had to tear all the fledgling, confusing emotions out before they took root and constricted and suffocated Ava. This time he would do the right thing. Wouldn't let the fallacy of love in. He'd mistaken other emotions for love— he wouldn't let Ava do the same and neither would he. Love was not in this.

'Liam.' Now she stood right in front of him, though he noted she was careful not to touch him, and once again he marvelled how soon their closeness, their ease and comfort together, had vanished. Perhaps he should take hope from that, that all these unwanted emotions would fade away with equal bleak rapidity. 'What did my mum say?'

'She wanted me to persuade you to over-throw the will.'

'What did you say?'

'I refused.'

Ava frowned. 'But what made her think you'd do it?'

'She thinks you love me, thinks I should use that love to further my ambition. That we could be happy together.'

Ava's eyes opened wide in shock and she stepped backwards and for a timeless instant silence reigned.

Ava's brain froze, became a dark cavernous void where any form of thought was impossible. She knew she needed to act, to refute the absurdity of his words, but somehow she couldn't figure out how. The right phrases simply wouldn't formulate on her tongue. Because her mother was right. Deep in her bones, in her soul, she could see the truth. She loved him.

For one tiny moment she considered telling him, allowed her imagination to picture it. For a moment rose-coloured spectacles came into play. He'd declare undying love, go down on one knee, roses and violins would feature...

Then she saw his face and the pink-tinged illusion dispersed to ash-coloured shadows. His expression was full of a concern that couldn't disguise the underlying mask of panic-stricken horror. That would be his worst nightmare: another woman in love with him who he didn't love back. This time a woman he didn't want to love back—at least Jess had had a fighting chance. But Liam would never love Ava, would never let himself take that risk, and so she would end up like her mother.

That would not happen. Ava would not walk the path her mother had chosen, where love became obsession and need, where you sacrificed pride and allowed love to warp into a twisted parody. So now she needed to pull out every single acting skill, every modelling trick she had ever learnt or used, and she would play her part down to the last detail. Would not let Liam know of her love.

Her incredulous laugh was pitched to perfection. 'Well, that poleaxed me. Love? That is ridiculous. Mum is clearly desperate for a new alliance. So she is seeing what she wants to see.' Liam's blue eyes studied her expression, scoured her face and Ava forced herself to remain loose limbed, to keep any hint of her true feelings from show. Shut down the writhe of panic and self-recrimination and pain that twisted inside her. And smiled her very best 'faking it' smile. After all, people believed what they wanted to believe and the smile had never let her down yet. 'I'm sorry it put you in an awkward position.'

'Don't worry about it. I'm glad it was a false alarm.'

'Of course it was. Our relationship is a charade. True, the parameters changed along the way, but love was never on the table.'

'No, it wasn't.' His voice was heavy and she hoped, how she hoped, he was buying her act.

'But now the dreaded L word has reared its head I think we'll both feel more comfortable if we wind the charade down.' There was no way she'd be able to be with him now, no way she could hold him, kiss him, fall asleep in his arms. Not now when she knew the dreadful truth.

'Agreed.' He nodded and she wondered what he was thinking, wanted him to say something, do something, tell her how he felt. But his expression was locked down and she forced herself not to ask. Knew she couldn't maintain this role much longer. She rose to her feet. 'Do you mind if we sort out technical details of how to deal with the press and roll out our break-up tomorrow? I think we need to phase out over the next few weeks, which means we will still have to see each other a bit. But perhaps we can plan some business trips, which will make it easier.'

'That sounds sensible. I'll sleep on the sofa and we'll regroup tomorrow.'

Ava nodded, knew that regrouping would not be possible for a very long time. But eventually her stupid foolish love would die. And until it did she'd pretend it had never existed—she could do that. Most supreme of ironies. She'd fake it till she made it. She was Ava Casseveti, after all.

CHAPTER SIXTEEN

LIAM PUT THE phone down, looked round his gleaming office and waited for the expected exultation to kick in. He'd won the Beaumont contract. Mission accomplished.

But the news felt...flat. Of course he was pleased—knew on a professional, practical level that his company was safe, was on its way up, and that did give him a deep sense of satisfaction. But the sense of victory he would have felt just weeks before was lacking. Now all he wanted was...to call Ava, to share the news. But he wouldn't because there would be no point.

Ava would say all the right things but... It wouldn't be real. He started to pace the office, in the hope that the monotonous strides would dull the ache of missing Ava. Because even though in the past two weeks they had seen each other, the meetings had been a true charade, a mockery of their previous closeness and camaraderie.

In truth it hadn't even felt like Ava—oh, the beautiful, perfectly dressed, perfectly poised woman had looked like Ava, sounded like Ava, but she had not been his Ava. His pace increased. Ava was not his, had never been his, could never be his.

He should be glad that she didn't love him, glad that she had been spared that hurt. Glad that she was able to continue to play her part now that the 'fun' was over. Yet perversely he wasn't… Because there was nothing to be glad about. A part of him wanted to go and find her, tell her he loved her. But how could he take that risk? He who knew his inability to navigate relationships. He couldn't figure out how to be part of a family in any sense. Not as a son, a stepbrother, a husband.

Yet now he recalled Ava's words.

'Do something about it. Stop being scared. I know I'm right. They wouldn't feel you were intruding, they'd welcome you in. It's your family unit.'

What if she were right? Before he could change his mind he picked up the phone.

'Mum?'

'Hello, Liam.'

'I was wondering if Max is there.'

'Max?' His mum sounded understandably confused.

'Yes. I wondered if he wanted to go skating.'

'I… I'm sure he'd love to. I'm about to drop him off to the rink anyway—it's one of his volunteer nights. Why don't you meet him there?'

'Great. I'll bring him back and maybe could we talk?'

'Of course.' A pause and, 'Are you OK?'

'Yes. I think so.'

Half an hour later Liam arrived at the roller-skating rink, aware of nerves and a sense of the surreal, aware that this 'everyday' activity felt like a step into the unknown.

'Liam. Hey.'

Max walked towards him, a shy smile on his face, and he realised that, despite his casual bearing, his stepbrother had been waiting for him.

'Hey. Hope this is OK.'

'Sure. It's cool. Mum says you'd like a skating lesson.'

'If that's OK with you?'

'Let's get you sorted with some skates and we can get started.' Max gave a sudden grin. 'I teach a group of four-year-olds some days… I'll give you the grown-up version.'

Liam pulled the skates on, watched as Max followed suit, saw how confident the teenager was. 'Right. Don't try to do too much too soon. To start with, balance against the wall and move how you can. Next you need to let go and waddle like a penguin.'

'Hey, what happened to the grown-up version?'

'I meant waddle like an adult penguin,' Max said, deadpan, and Liam gave a snort of laughter.

'Like this?'

'Perfect.'

'OK. Whilst I practise my waddle, why don't you show me how it's really done?'

'Sure.' And then he was off, and Liam's jaw dropped as he watched Max weave in and out of the throng of customers in an incredible display of speed and agility before zooming back.

'That was incredible.' Liam shook his head. 'I know there's no way I'll ever be able to do that, but if you could coach me so I can at least do a circuit that would be great.' He glanced around. 'I know you're working too.'

He watched, saw how professional Max and the other skate guards were, watched the speed skating and realised Max had a real talent. And throughout Max came and offered encouragement and help until, 'I've got it,' Liam crowed.

'You have. You've clicked. Now it's all

about practice and I'm pretty sure you'll get up to a good speed in no time.'

Liam held out a hand. 'Thanks, Max. You've been great. I appreciate it.'

By the end of the evening Liam had a happy sense of achievement, felt a connection to Max that he genuinely hoped to build on.

'Did you have fun?' Bea asked as they arrived back.

'It was cool,' Max said as he headed upstairs.

'Definitely cool,' Liam agreed.

'You said you wanted to talk,' Bea said. 'John's still at work.'

'That's fine. I… I just wanted some advice, I guess.' The idea was strange.

'About Ava?'

'Yes. How did you know?'

'I saw Ava a couple of days ago.'

'For drinks with Anna Lise. How was it?'

'It was fun. It was lovely of Ava to organise it. But Ava and I stayed and had a last drink and I got the feeling something isn't quite right between you. She said you're thinking of having a break.'

'Yes.' That was the story they'd agreed on, a kind of phased break-up. Pain jabbed at him and he tried to remind himself that you couldn't break up something that had never existed in the first place. 'But I don't want a break.'

'Then tell her.'

'It's not that easy.'

'Why not?'

'I'm scared.' The admission was terrifying in itself. 'I've always messed up relationships. I don't know how to do it.'

'So you're just going to give up? Throw away a chance for true happiness?'

'Like you did for me?'

'I am happy, Liam.'

'You are now. But you weren't—you spent years trapped in an unhappy marriage. Wasted years. Because of me.' Just like Jess had wasted her precious years. With him.

'No.' Pain touched Bea's eyes. 'That is not how it was, Liam. I stayed because I wanted to, because it was the right thing to do. For you and for me. Terry was your dad. He loved you. In the end I couldn't take you away from him. That was my choice and I've never regretted it. I loved you. I still love you. You were my priority and I do not regret that choice. If what happened then, between your dad and me, between you and me, is affecting your decisions now, then please don't let it. I know your marriage to Jess was both complex and tragic. But don't let that stop you now. Don't let what happened in the past take away from you and Ava.'

'There is no me and Ava. There can't be. I can't take the risk I'll mess it up again. It's not fair to her.'

'It doesn't work like that. Don't you think Ava deserves to make that choice for herself? Make her own risk assessment? Don't take that away from her.'

After all, wasn't that what he'd done to Jess? Not told the truth. Not given her a choice. Made assumptions.

'Think about it,' she said. 'Please.'

'I will.' Without hesitation he rose, could almost see the air clear between them as he moved over to her and hugged her. 'And thank you.'

Ava looked round, wondered if she'd lost her mind, imagined the wrath of her mother, the wrath of her lawyers if they knew her current whereabouts. She slouched down, pulled the brim of the designer sunhat a little further down and cast a furtive glance at the Italian offices, the headquarters of Luca Petrovelli's business.

Diligent research had uncovered an interview where he'd said he sometimes liked to eat his lunch in a nearby park—so here she was staking out the premises for the second day in a row. It at least gave her something to focus on apart from Liam, provided a small distraction from the pain that weighted her cracked heart.

She looked at the revolving door one more time and blinked in disbelief. There was Luca—in truth, she'd not really anticipated success. So now what?

Better to trail him to the park or he might simply turn and retreat back into his fortress or, worse, call security on her. Trying not to look furtive, she followed her half-brother until he seated himself on a bench. Her insides clenched with trepidation and swiftly she headed towards him and sat down. Cast a sideways glance at him. Dark hair presumably inherited from his mother. Grey eyes, ditto. But his nose was their dad's, and his lips, and she could see something of herself in him, something elusive that she couldn't quite place. Something that made them kin.

Now she was staring and Luca turned.

'Luca?' Ava heard the smallness of her voice.

'If you are a reporter I have noth—' He broke off as grey eyes met amber. He paled under the olive skin, and she felt the shock of recognition. 'Ava?'

'Yes.'

For a full minute they just sat and looked at each other, the birds in the background, the noise of the breeze rustling the trees. Ava locked the moment away—no matter what happened next, she'd done this, looked for Luca and found him, and now she needed to say what she had come to say. 'I'm sorry to surprise you like this but it seemed important we talk, in private, face to face.'

'But not here. We could be spotted. Come. We'll find a café, somewhere busy and anonymous.'

Once in a bustling café redolent with the smell of pastries and hot chocolate and percolating coffee, he turned to her.

'What would you like?'

'Black coffee and an almond croissant.'

His smile was tight. 'Jodi's favourite.' The words jolted her, the idea that she shared something with a sister she'd never met.

Once back at the table he sat down and stared at her, his face unsmiling, his eyes hard. 'So why are you here?'

'Because the whole talking through lawyers isn't working. Because I need to know what you want to do about Dolci. Because I wanted to see you. Meet you, even if it's only once.'

His gaze didn't waver. 'Do your lawyers know you're here?'

'No. No one knows I'm here.' And only one man wouldn't condemn her for it. For an instant she wished Liam were here, waiting at the hotel. Someone to have her back. But that wasn't to be. Couldn't be. 'Truly. I just want to know what you and Jodi want.'

A shadow crossed his face and then he leant back. 'How about you tell me what you want?'

'I'd like to figure out a way for us all to work together. As a family. You, me and Jodi. I know there will be tensions and difficulties. And obstacles. But we could find a way to overcome them.'

'That won't be so easy.'

'I know. My mother—she will oppose this and I don't know how your mother will react. I don't know the answers. But I would like to try and figure them out with you and Jodi.'

Now Luca sighed. 'OK. I believe you. Though my own lawyers will have a hissy fit. But there is another problem. One you don't know about.'

Liam stood at the arrivals gate, his eyes scanning the travellers as they came through, some weary, some with smiles as they looked for their loved ones. His whole body was wired as if he'd drunk a bath full of caffeine; anticipation and terror tingled through him at the thought of seeing Ava. Then there she was, blonde hair pulled back in a ponytail, dressed in a cable-knit sweater, jeans and boots, tugging a suitcase behind her.

He knew that her nails were probably accessorised to her luggage and the idea tugged at something deep inside him. His heart cartwheeled at the sheer joy of seeing her even as nerves nearly caused him to remain out of her line of vison, flat-footed and petrified.

Swiftly he strode forward, stepped into her path. 'Ava.'

Her eyes widened and for a second there was his Ava. Her eyes held a fleeting happiness—joy, even—and then the emotion muted, vanished and he wondered if he had simply seen what he wanted with all his heart to see. 'Liam. What are you doing here?'

'I came to pick you up. I wanted to see you.' He'd vowed to tell the truth, not play with words or act a part, yet he didn't want to spook her, wanted to do this right. But the words of love wanted to escape right here and now and he swallowed them down. Better to stick to plan, maintain hope for longer. 'If you're not exhausted I thought we could talk. Off script. If you are tired I'll drop you off home.'

'I'm not exhausted or even tired. I'd like to talk.' That sideways glance, her amber eyes flecked with curiosity.

'Good. Let's go somewhere more private.'

'Sure.' They walked to the car in silence, Liam simply happy to be with her, to have her close in this moment when he could still hope.

'Where are we going?'

'It's a surprise.'

Now a small smile tipped her lips and then vanished, replaced by a frown. 'Have I forgotten something? Is this part of our break-up plan?'

God, he hoped not. Nerves tautened inside him. *Jeez. Show some backbone, Rourke.* Worst-case scenario, he'd get hung out to dry, be humiliated. But he'd have been honest. He'd be able to look back without regret. There would be no what ifs to haunt either of them. 'We're here.' It didn't answer her question but it'd do.

Nerves crackled through him as he pulled to the kerb outside the London park. He climbed out and saw Rita and her boyfriend parked close behind him. The petite redhead waved, jumped out of her car, opened her boot and he walked over to heft the hamper out. He'd wanted the food to be chilled and the wine to be cold.

'Here you go. I'll drive the car back to the garage.' Rita caught the keys he tossed to her and turned to Ava. 'He chose it all himself. I'm just the delivery girl.' She stepped closer to him. 'Good luck, Big Guy.'

He'd take any luck going, though somehow the jangle of his nerves had calmed now his plan was under way, now he was committed to his course of action. Ava followed him through the park until they reached the place he'd chosen. He pulled open the basket, took out the portable heater and the thick tweed blanket, spread it on the ground. The late afternoon sunshine still touched the ground and air with a touch of early spring warmth but he knew soon enough the late March evening would turn colder.

Ava watched and he saw realisation dawn in her eyes. 'It's our first date,' she said. 'The one we couldn't have.'

'Because it wouldn't have been the right time of year,' he said. 'I am hoping that now is. The right time for a real first date. Not part of a charade or a pretence. Or an imaginary projection. Real. With a real blanket and a real hamper.' He gestured towards the wicker basket. 'I have chilled white wine. I have crystal flutes.'

'And soon there will be stars in the sky and we can sit and talk and...'

'Discuss the constellations.'

'And it will be magical.'

'Yes. Because I think we're good at magic. I want a chance for us to do this properly, to win your love the right way. If that's what you want.' *Stop talking, Rourke.* 'If it isn't, then that's OK too. I'll get it. Please don't go along with this because you don't want to hurt me.' He knew the damage that could be done that way.

'Love?' Her voice held surprise, shock, but also perhaps an undertone of hope.

'I love you, Ava.' He tried for a smile. 'I know it's a bit forward on a first date and I am not expecting you to reciprocate.'

She stepped forward, put her hand on his arm, her face, oh, so serious. 'I won't lie to you, Liam. Not now. Not ever. So I swear to you that what I am about to say is the truth The whole truth and nothing but the truth. I love you too.'

For a moment he stared at her, unable to believe the words, but then he took in her expression, the love in her eyes, the happiness that illuminated her smile, a smile that he knew was real. And a sense of joyous disbelief dawned inside him, pulled an incredulous chuckle. 'You love me?'

'Yes.'

'So you love me and I love you?'

'Yes.' Now her smile widened. 'This is the best first date ever.' She sank down onto the blanket and he followed suit, busied himself with switching the heater on, and then she snuggled next to him. Moved away, studied his expression. 'You are sure, aren't you?'

'Yes, I am. One hundred per cent and then some. This is real, Ava. And, hell, it frightened me. That's why I fought it for so long. Because I was so scared I couldn't handle it. Just like I couldn't handle my parents' relationship, just like I messed up my marriage. I thought the safest path was one I walked alone.'

'So you couldn't hurt anyone else.' Her voice was gentle now, so full of warmth and understanding. 'What changed your mind?'

'You. You've changed me, Ava, made me see things I couldn't before. I did make mistakes, but I don't have to bear all the responsibility. I have accepted that other people make choices too. My mum made her own decisions, so did Jess. She was part of our marriage too and she made mistakes as well.'

Ava shifted even closer to him, laid her

head against his shoulder, and the tickle of her corn-blonde hair, her closeness, filled him with joy. 'You showed me that I don't need to cut myself off from everyone. You were right about my mum, about John and Max. They are my family. I've spent a lot of time with them in the past days. Max took me skating.'

'Really?' Now she laughed, the sound melodious and light in the evening air.

'Yup. Apparently I'm a natural. For someone of my advanced years. Something else I wouldn't have discovered if it weren't for you.'

Ava grinned at him. 'Well, you've done wonders for me too. Guess what happened on my business trip.'

'Tell me.'

'Well, I went to Italy to see Leonardo Brunetti and we signed the deal.'

'Ava, that is fantastic!'

'It gets better.' Her eyes sparked with happiness, her expressive face catching the light of the setting sun. 'I also saw Luca.'

He took her hands in his, held tight, knew how much courage that must have taken. 'You are incredible. How was it?'

'Amazing. Surreal. I can't believe I finally met him and there was an instant definite connection. And you were right. The reason he hasn't been in contact properly isn't because he hates me or that he is vindictive. It's because he really doesn't know what Jodi wants. He doesn't even know where she is.'

'She's missing?'

'No. She just won't tell Luca where she is. After Dad died Jodi took off to go travelling. Luca said she was having a great time and then suddenly she changed. Contact lessened and now she's asked him to leave her alone, promised that she is OK and she doesn't want him to pull his "big brother shit". He is really worried. It sounds like they are really close. But he won't make any decisions on Dolci without her.'

'That makes sense and I hope Jodi is OK. And I am so glad you have begun to sort things out with Luca.'

'Me too. We decided that for now I'll keep running the company but I'll keep him in the loop. We'll talk, conference call and he will have some input. Once Jodi is back in the picture properly we'll go from there. I even spoke to Mum, told her what I'd done. She wasn't happy but I did tell her that no matter what happens I will always be there for her. That I want her to be part of my life. But I realise that she will have to make that choice. And she didn't shoot me down in flames and she's agreed to hold fire on trying to overturn the will herself So I hope that we'll work it out. I know it will take time but I have hope.'

'I am so pleased for you.' And he was, knew how much this meant to her.

'But it's thanks to you I did it. You've shown me how to be me, to stop playing a part, to stop trying to please everyone else without taking my own views into account. You've shown me my opinion does count. You listened to me, encouraged and supported my ideas. That's one of the reasons I fell in love with you.'

He grinned at her. 'What were the others?'

'You make me laugh, you're loyal and caring and honourable and with you I can be myself.'

'Always.' He cupped her cheek. 'Because I love you for you. I love the way you smile, the way you care about everyone, the way you deal with difficult situations. I love that you have fun, take selfies. I love you, Ava. I want to wake up with you beside me every day. I want to be at your side for the ups and the downs. I want to have children with you, to grow old with you.'

'That's what I want too. You've shown me that love can be a good thing, a beautiful thing. That it isn't all about need or obsession. It's about a partnership, about reciprocity, about being there for each other. It's not a power struggle, it's about two people who want to be together, who work through their problems together. Because I know that's what we'll do.' Her gaze encompassed him with love and he felt an awe and wonder. 'For ever.'

'For ever.'

Then he kissed her, a kiss that sealed their love, marked the beginning of for ever. A kiss that filled him with pure happiness that this woman loved him. And so they spent their first date, began their for ever, lying under the stars and planning their future.

* * * * *

Look out for the next story in
The Casseveti Inheritance trilogy
Coming soon!

And if you enjoyed this story,
check out these other great reads
from Nina Milne

Baby on the Tycoon's Doorstep
Their Christmas Royal Wedding
Whisked Away by Her Millionaire Boss

All available now!